POISONED LOVE

Can Nina unravel the truth behind the deception and Betrayal before it's too late? Will, Will be able to trust his own heart and the love that blooms between him and Nina, or will the shadows of his past destroy their chance at happiness?

In a race against tie and hose who seek to destroy him, Will must confront his own demons and fight for the love and future he desperately desires. Deception and betrayal lurk around every corner, but with Nina by his side, Will may just find the strength to overcome it all and reclaim his life.

Once every so often the world hears a new voice. Mosley Van Norman is the person to whom that voice belongs.

— THAT GUY WHO'S ALWAYS AT STARBUCKS

Mosley Van Norman

POISONED LOVE

A WRITER'S AMNESIA A DOCTORS AFFECTION

MOSLEY VAN NORMAN

Copyright © 2024 by Mosley Van Norman

All rights reserved.

No part of this book may be reproduced in any form or by any electronic or mechanical means, including information storage and retrieval systems, without written permission from the author, except for the use of brief quotations in a book review.

❦ Created with Vellum

1

Nina

"Don't even," I say, clasping my hands on Claire's shoulders and guiding her away from the large gate.

"Don't even what?" She responds with a firm glare, trying to resist the pull.

"Don't even think about it. The house is off-limits to everybody else, well, except its residents."

"Why's that?"

Before I could respond to her question, I turn away from the gate and head towards the car, "Well, I heard that the owner of the house, who's over ninety years old, has amnesia. Looks like there's a big bag of secrets engulfing the house and its occupants. But..." I say, turning to Claire. "It could just be hearsay and nothing more. So, forget I said that."

"Really? If you know so much, why haven't you

approached them with your skills yet? Who knows, working for them just might fetch you some fortune." She adds with a shrug.

I take a moment to consider the question. *Not a bad proposition after all...*

INDEED, I had never thought about that because, in my defense, you know how your mind and brain automatically default to a situation after learning about something? That's what happened to me. I had heard that the house was off-limits, and I suddenly forgot who I was, but I wasn't ready to tell her that just yet. Instead, I change the subject almost immediately. "What do you know about amnesiac patients?"

"You know, I know barely anything about them. You're the doctor, not me, remember? Claire replies, almost annoyed.

"Oh! There's so much to say, but how do I explain this...?" I start off, chuckling.

Claire shot me a pissed-off glare, then sprinted towards the car, with me following close.

"Oh, come on, don't be like this. Suck it up," I coaxed, but she didn't budge.

I was in the midst of resolving the conflict with my friend when my landlord appeared out of the blue. He was a middle-aged man, maybe somewhere in his forties. But you couldn't miss the guy, especially not with his long, cylindrical face and piercing blue eyes.

Quite frankly, I thought he had the possibility of being cute if he didn't always wear that grumpy expression and I know, I am most certainly not the most attractive women in the world. In fact, I have never really considered myself a pretty lady. I mean, I have my wrinkles, but that doesn't mean I have an inferiority complex. I'm four feet twelve, with mid length brunette hair and olive eyes. I've never considered myself pretty, at least not with my insanely freckled face.

"Nina, a word?" says my landlord. *Not even a hello? Geez.*

"Hello, Kent."

My dad always told me to greet a jackass, but I never thought it worked on Kent. He never learned that lesson too well.

"You do remember that you have to pay your outstanding dues, correct?"

"Yeah, I haven't forgotten. I was going to see you next weekend."

"We better make it this weekend and this weekend only." He says, walking off.

With a slouch, I look out, only to see my mom in action, looking out the window like a creepy peeping Tom. I resisted the urge to roll my eyes.

Things haven't really gone as planned for as long as I can remember, and I face the risk of eviction if I can't pay off my rent, and from all indications, I may not have the money.

"What's the problem, bitch?" Claire asks from inside the car, assessing the tensed look on my face. As soon as I snap of my reverie, I look back her way, hesitating to respond.

"Oh...uh. I'm fine. Nothing to worry about." I reply, turning to her with a smile.

"Stop that. We've known each other for God knows how long. So, you very well know that you're hiding something," she says calmly, as if reading my mind.

"Come on, stop acting like a twelve-year-old." I scolded, giving her a light tug on the shoulder. "It's just the same old story, nothing new," I add with a grumpy shrug. After this, we both remain silent for a painful couple of minutes before I start the engine.

Pouring out my heart to Claire on such occasions was like intentionally setting myself up for disaster. But...it wasn't because she took out the worse in me but rather because I felt myself clamming up, sinking deeper into my worries. Also, she does have an awful habit of going on and on with so much enthusiasm, while I listened on like she was making a lot of sense which she actually didn't most of the time. It's what best friends do anyway, we make our friends feel like they're in that ephemeral moment where they're Mother Teresa, offering ethereal wisdom that could change the fucking universe when in reality, it makes no sense in your head.

However, Claire and I go way back. We have been friends since high school and she is the only one still in my corner. No one else has ever gone out of their way for me like Claire, not even my mother. Heck, Claire even knocked some fashion sense into me, especially when I was struggling some mornings to put on a cute look for some random guy in one of my classes. So, there was absolutely no point in trying to impress her.

Pushing all these jumbled thoughts aside, I drive through university city down market street to my clinic located at 61st and Spruce still not saying anything to Claire. The sixteen-minute drive to my clinic, which was usually a refreshing, felt like a slow trip to Nirvana this morning all thanks to Kent, who just had to remind me of my debt.

When we arrive at the clinic, Claire I go our separate ways.

"Goodbye, baby," she says before turning away. But a step later, turns back, "Oh and don't trip, girl. It's going to be alright." She says with a nudge.

"Aww, look at you. You can be sweet sometimes," I say with a squeal. "Catch you later."

I watched her throttle down the lane, becoming smaller before disappearing. Then, I make my way into the clinic. It was a small, but cozy unit, with brightly colored walls, child-friendly artwork, and lots of toys and books. The exam rooms were decorated with kid-friendly themes, with separate areas for older kids, and a separate waiting area for parents. Back then, when the place was always buzzing with patients, I used to boast of the friendly and caring staff. Those were my days because there were no inpatients in the clinic that morning. The last had been discharged the night before, so that meant I was less busy, and my receptionist, well, she was already bored out of her wit, and in a way, I felt sorry for her.

"Nina! Good morning!" Says Joyce as soon as I enter her sight.

"Oh! You're in early, good morning!" I say before staring at the clock on the wall. This woman literally came in 30 minutes before she was supposed to—that's crazy to me.

"Ah well. Let's just say I felt a bit strange this morning, so I came in to distract myself." She says with a bit of apprehension.

"Something wrong at home?"

Joyce and I had "that kind" of relationship. We became close friends after every other person left, leaving us to pick up the crumbs behind them. I was grateful she'd stayed, it meant so much to me and the clinic, obviously.

"I think I'm pregnant." She says, with a sad look.

"What?" I ask, walking closer to where she was sitting, "Isn't that a good thing?"

Joyce had a well-off boyfriend who lived downtown in a luxurious condo, something some of us could only dream of at least here in the city where prices for literally gum was astronomical.

"Isn't Charles ready to take responsibility? I mean, for starters, does he even know you are carrying his child?"

"It's not that." She says, completely dismissing my second question.

"Then what?" I ask, genuinely concerned.

"You know, I'm not sure if I want to keep this baby. I need more, I deserve more. I need to live my life, be independent. I have no inkling of what tomorrow's going to be like. Nothing is for certain, Nina, and that's what scares me. How do I even begin to think about bringing a child into this?" Joyce heaved, trembling slightly.

I am the the last person to offer relationship advice, but I try my best. I've had pregnancy scares cross my mind a ton of times, and I felt like giving her the advice that I would've wanted to hear if I were in her place.

"It's okay to feel that way. You're going to be a mother soon, you're going to bring a life into this world and it's a huge responsibility, but what matters is that you're not alone. You have Charles, you have your family, and you have me, duh. I'll always be here," I say with a cocky yet playful smile.

"Thank you, Nina." She responds with giving my hand a slight squeeze.

"Seems like it's settled now, so no more sad faces, or I'll jump into the Schuylkill River," I say, and we both laugh

Just as I was about the head the other direction, to get started on what I really came into the office for, Larry barges in. He had recently bought some properties around a popular, commercial area, one of which I was using for my very own clinic.

"Hey, Larry."

"Hello ladies. Nina, I need a word with you, it shouldn't take long." He says as he ushers me away from Joyce.

"Business doesn't look good these days." He says in his usual airy voice, glancing around the place.

"Well, I agree. We've seen better days," I replied, walking him to my office, hoping he would agree to a sit-down.

"Don't bother, as I said, this won't take long," he says before continuing, "I called your home number; your mom can fill you in on everything from here." *What the hell was that supposed to mean?*

"What? You called my mom? Why?" I asked, exasperated.

"Oh, I didn't know talking to your mom was off the table for me, sweetcakes." He says in a sarcastic tone that made me rage on the inside.

"What the fuck, Larry? You have no idea what you've thrown me into." I harrumphed, packing my bag and car key, and making my way out the door with Larry behind. We walked past Joyce at the counter, and didn't say a word. I can't blame her, I guess she knew what was at stake already.

"Stop. We haven't discussed why I came to see you."

"No, Larry. I think you've done enough harm for one day."

"Look at you, sly little girl. Is this your elaborate way to escape rent?"

"Escape paying my rent? Are you for real?" I say, completely disgusted by him at this point.

"Fine, I see talking to you will get me nothing at this point, so just go, but remember, we'll have this conversation again," Larry said.

I slam the door angrily behind him and make my way to the house. Being at work was not the best place to be at my current mental state, but I knew what nightmare awaited me because of Larry's pettiness.

My drive home took shorter than usual because I drove like a maniac, and when I got home, my nightmare was waiting. I wasn't tiptoeing, but it felt like I was, as I crept into the house feeling like a mouse in a meeting with giant beasts, only the giant was my mom. As soon as I enter the living room, she shoots me a stern look, watching me like a hawk eyeing its prey. Heck, I kid you not, you could cut the tension in the room with a knife.

"I know you have something to say, so I will give you a couple minutes."

"Don't push it, you know you won't like what I have to say." My mom replies with a snappy attitude. I'm fucking twenty-four and my mother treats me like I'm in my early teen era.

"It's okay. Wouldn't make any difference now, nor hurt more, I'm so used to your antics already, if you couldn't tell." In all honesty, I used to be afraid of her, pray as if it's my last day on earth when I knew she would have to confront me about something, but at this point, I was just so numb to everything. I didn't care.

"No, you listen to me, lady. You have no kids, so you have no inkling how heartbreaking it feels to watch your child sink deep into the sand."

There was a brief moment of silence, then my mom heaved a deep sigh that said a lot even before she said anything.

"Larry called." *Ahah! There, she finally mentioned that son of a bitch.*

"I know, what did he say?"

"You know." She replied, sliding into the chair behind her. Mom had arthritis; she actually had been suffering from it for the past seven years and was on nonsteroidal anti-inflammatory drugs. I needed all the money I could get. She was my only family left, and I needed her alive. Not being capable of doing all of those made me feel incapacitated like I was stuck in a rut.

"I'm going to pay him off soon, mom." I assured.

"By doing what, huh? Selling corn flour or molly in your clinic?"

"Mom, chill. What do you rather I do?"

"Get a job elsewhere. It wouldn't hurt to work in a community hospital, would it?"

"But... what's going to happen to my clinic?"

"Think about what you're saying, Nina. Your clinic won't put food on the table. It can't even fetch you anything right now, you can always ditch it. I'm trying to help here." She added, after a while, softening slightly.

"No, ma, you're not helping. You know what, we shouldn't have this conversation." I said, taking a bow.

2

Will

The roars and cheers kept resounding in my ears as I sat glancing from one corner of the hall to the other. That had to be my biggest signing meeting ever, and the numbers never diminished. It just felt never-ending, especially when I looked up to see the entrance. At intervals, I had to resist the urge to scream "I love London!"

"That's a wrap on the question-and-answer segment. Time for you to meet your fans now." Lily says into my ears. She had been my personal assistant ever since I started this gig. In fact, she is the one who persuaded me to go down this rabbit hole ever since we were in college, and it has got to be the best decision I've ever made.

"Thanks," I replied, heading down the podium to the trailhead of the foyer where fans were already queued up.

"That was a great job by the way." She whispered again, and I nodded.

Peering across the five thousand-capacity auditorium, The Royal Albert Hall, named after Queen Victoria's husband, Prince Albert at the thousands of bodies queued up to get an autograph felt so...thrilling. I could feel the adrenaline rush through my body.

The stunning interior, dome-shaped ceiling, intricate murals, grand chandelier, and the ornate decorations were just the elegant scenario I'd envisioned. Not to mention, a big kudos to the bouncers, they were at their best to keep everyone coordinated in the large foyer as they wait for their turn.

Sitting in such a beautiful and historic venue with my fans, with the chandeliers beaming up in the ceiling, I felt kind of strangely connected to my fans. I felt this nostalgic feeling, like of knights in the palace and emperors. *Now...this was inspiration for my next big book.*

Hunched in one of the seats was Lily, my assistant. She smiled as our eyes interlocked, giving me the thumbs up for motivation, and I nodded in response.

We'd gone over possible interview questions in Philadelphia, and it had been amazing how much my fans yearned to know about me—nothing was off the table for them. They asked me questions about my personal life, such as any love interests to more generic questions like if I would start a complete series for the book. I don't blame them; the stories were left on exciting cliff hangers. The ask-and-answer session was just too fun that I'd forgotten what we'd planned initially, all I saw was an ocean of people who didn't need to get close to me but could care about me from where they stood.

It felt warm.

"What would you like for me to address?" I asked a little girl who looked giddy.

"My mom. She is crazy over you, not like in a b-bad way. She made me read your books, and I fell in l-love with your stories, too."

"Wow! That's amazing. Where is your mom if you don't mind me asking?" I ask, calmly.

Her jaw dropped, and her face turned pale. "She... passed." She replies, her tone sad and hushed.

I bit my lower lip as my chest tightened. I'd thought she was trying to save face, but I'd ended up hurting her feelings.

"I'm so sorry." I said, meaning it. "I didn't mean to..."

"No, it's fine." She replies, hastily. "I'm glad I finally got to meet you. I've made one of her dreams come true, so I hope she will be happy in the afterlife." She said, the smile reappearing on her face.

This young girl just made my heart melt and it truly felt like the best thing I'd heard in so long.

"What's your name?"

"Margaret." She replied.

"Tell me, Margaret, what do you think I could do to make your mom happy?"

She flushed excitedly, and without any form of hesitancy, she belched, "Don't stop writing. I hate the wait, but I don't mind waiting, as long as you give me an ethereal book to jump on. I want to read your books for a very long time!" She replied, hurriedly.

"Then I shall keep writing," I assured, and she giggled off.

I followed her with my eyes, fascinated by her strength and decorum. Considering how numb I'd felt after Grandpa Declan died, I think the little girl was strong, much stronger than she looked.

"Next please," I announced, but as the next person

stepped forward, I heard the familiar buzz from a distance, and I knew the catastrophe that was whirling towards me. It's usually difficult to decide what happens afterwards, but I'm certain that my crew did a great job of coming up with a good enough excuse to conceal the embarrassment and keep the ball rolling.

∽

I SIT BACK in my seat on the private jet that was now on route to New York, taking a sip of the hard scotch. But I couldn't help as my mind kept jolting back to the fan signing, and my blackout. I'd watched the video, and so far, there was no criticism from fans, looks like no one observed the change in behavior. Was I that incredible at coordination? What if they recognized it, but only chose to stay silent so that they don't hurt my feelings?

Nothing could stay concealed forever, that I know of, and I must admit, there were moments I perceived that they knew what demon I was battling with. I wasn't soliciting their sympathy, but I so badly wanted to tell my fans the truth. I shouldn't keep secrets from them, but in a way, it was better if some things remained hidden. I needed them to see me as the tough and creative writer they all thought I was... and am.

Lily spiraled past me down the aisle, setting our bags and preparing some appetizers, or so I'd thought. Seeing her reminded me of her role at the fan signing. She was amazing, as usual. Lily always managed to make even the most mundane tasks seem like a walk in the park. Not just that, her beauty was undeniable, with her long, dark hair and piercing green eyes, she was an incredibly beautiful woman, but I knew better than to ruin the professional and cordial relationship we had going on. However, despite that, I couldn't deny the chemistry between us. I knew she had a thing for me or else why would we yearn for each other and crave that intimacy at every second we have alone? Not that she had no will, I would never bed her against her will.

Just like that, my mind drifts away and I start to remember all the moments we shared together. We'd both done crazy things at dangerous places and times. Hell, I recall fucking her in the bathroom of my son's school restroom. I can't remember what the fuck I was on, but I'd been horny all through my journey to Caleb's school, and I'd gone into the men's room to relieve myself. Lily had accompanied me to grab my boy since we had been in a conference just moments earlier, she knocked on the door, scared I'd blacked out again, and my hormones just took over. I grabbed her and well...we fucked. There was no sugar coating it. To be honest, her assistance and role in my career was commensurable, the more reason she was at the top of my payroll.

There were so many questions to ask, and so many things to do, but as I gazed out the window of the plane, still enveloped with thoughts of the fan signing, I felt a tap on my shoulder. I swirled around to see Lily standing by with a look of concern on her face.

"Is everything alright?" she asks, her voice low and husky.

I hesitated for a moment, contemplating a response, "Everything's fine. Just a lot on my mind." She nodded and smiled.

"Well, I'm here if you need me, sir." She stressed the last part, with her hand tangling her hair, and I recognized that gesture. I'd seen that before, and I knew exactly what it meant.

The plane suddenly experienced turbulence, and she stumbled into my chest. *How fucking corny.* "Oh my God. I'm s-sorry about that," she said, trying to regain her footing. But she was having trouble getting up, and I felt my cock harden. She looked up at me, her face just inches from mine, but I looked at her with no expression on my face, aware of the level of testosterone accumulating within me.

Then I watched as recognition set in, she'd recognized that I wasn't ready to take the first step, so she crouched on her knees. Running her hands down my zipper trail. She raised her face to my level, curling her lips, while her hands fondled and pulled down my zipper. She grazed her hands over my already stiff cock and pulled down my pants and briefs.

"You're hard," she says, stating the obvious as she slipped my shaft into her perfect mouth. I struggled to retain the groan that begged to splurge out from my mouth as the action built sexual tension in my body.

She suckled gently, moaning lowly, and then increased the pace, sucking rougher. Instinctively, my hands grabbed a fistful of her hair, shoving my cock deeper down her throat as she gaggled, sucking deeper.

"Damnit." I groaned, letting out a shaky breath and feeling my body temperature rise.

My hands reach down her blouse, aggressively grabbing on to her tender boob and even harder nipples.

Lily threw her head back, breathing heavily, my cock falling out of her mouth for a slight second, but she was soon on it, sucking hungrily as my hands ran down to her boobs, massaging and spanking in rhythm.

Taking a standing position, she pulled off her blouse, exposing her perfect breast, the sight of which got me even more taut as I struggled to contend the urge to shove my cock into her tight little pussy. *I needed her, fuck.*

She sat on my lap, offering her perky nipple to me as happily took it into my mouth and judging by the sounds she let out, I knew she was enjoying herself.

"I want to fuck you," I whispered as a matter-of-fact into her ear, and a smirk creased her face.

"So, what are you waiting for, sir?" She teased, rousing from my lap, and settling on the soft leather seat across from me, with her legs spread apart.

I rush towards her, removing my shirt, which was the only piece of clothing I had on and tossing them toward the end of the plane. Tucking her skirt up to her waist, my fingers ran eagerly, filing her panties and dragging them down as I tugged in a finger, feeling her wet pussy coat my fingers.

"You're so fucking wet, too." I teased.

"Mhm. For you," she responds, her tone laced with lust.

I give her a tough glare, enjoying her enthusiasm. "Well, let me take care of you then." I scowl, and deliver exactly as promised.

Without protection, I shove my hard cock into her with a single thrust, cocking my head to the side as the soft music played in my head. She was already soaking wet, so it wasn't the hardest task in the world to enter her, thankfully, because where the fuck would I find lube on in this plane.

Wrapping her legs around my waist, she gave my back a tug, urging me to go harder, "Come on baby, harder, I need it!"

Settling in between her thighs, I cupped her boobs in my hands, caressing one, and suckling on the other. Then with another thrust, I breached her walls, romping slowly, then increased the pace. I didn't care about the other men she could potentially be screwing alongside me, but I needed her to know that no man could fuck her better than I did. Her light moan grew steadily into a whimper, then a cry for more and more.

"Is that hard enough, huh?" I ask, romping hard, but she was stubborn.

"Harder." She repeated, fueling me with the desire to make her reach her orgasm. My pace doubled as I jerked in and out, breathless. As her mouth went open, and a smile formed on her pretty face, I watched her convulse, splurging creamy discharge on my cock.

I let her some seconds, then romped in again, this time thrusting much more aggressively, hearing the sound of her wet cunt echo like percussion in my ear.

"Yes, yes, yes." She chorused. Then raising her hands to her boobs, she caressed them aggressively before her left hand traveled down to her folds, where she massaged fiercely while moaning deeply. With my hand on her waist, I thrust in a final time, jerking, and groaning at every inch of pleasure. Each romp was hard and steady, until we climaxed.

3

Nina

"Hello, Dr. Nina. This is Leslie Reynolds from Telehealth Insurance company. I'm calling to discuss your claim," says the other voice in a calm yet professional manner.

I took a deep breath and prepared myself mentally for what was sure to be a frustrating conversation. As much as I'd been looking forward to it, I knew deep in my bones that I was equally dreading the truth.

"Hello. Thank you for calling. Go ahead." I say, my voice tinged with fear.

"I'm afraid we're not able to cover the full amount of your losses in your current situation. Your policy doesn't cover the amount of damage you incur on bankruptcy."

"But that's impossible!" I protest. "My clinic is on the verge of closing if I can't pay off my debt. I'll lose everything...my equipment, supplies, patient records - and you're telling me you can't cover the costs?" I rant on.

"I'm sorry, Dr. Nina. It's not a question of desire; it's a question of policy. I understand this is frustrating, but there's nothing I can do. You'll need to file a claim with the state government for assistance." Leslie's voice was firm.

I felt my blood boiling as I listened to her voice on the phone, my thoughts swirling, searching for alternatives.

"You can't be serious!" I exclaimed. "How would I recover from this?" I ask, but Leslie's tone remained cool and collected.

"I understand your frustration, Dr. Nina, but you didn't include this particular condition in your claims, so I hope you understand why there isn't much we can do on our end. We are also not authorized to approve your claim at this moment." She took a short pause, during which I thought she was going to return with hopeful news, but she shattered the remaining pieces of hope I was clinging on to.

"I really wish we could help you, but we're unable to, and I apologize about that. I'm just following the policy guidelines. I know this is difficult for you. Is there anything else I can help you with?" She asked, completely changing the subject.

I paused, trying in vain to compose myself. "No, I guess not," I finally replied. "Thank you for your time," I said half-heartedly, and she hung up.

My hands went to my face as I tried to push back the steaming tears that were building in my eyes. Sprinting to my feet, I move over to the window and pull the blinds down; I just wanted to shut myself out.

Later that day, I'd laid off Joyce. It was such a terrible thing to do, but I had no other choice. It was either that or have her work for free, which I would never do regardless, but especially now that she was pregnant. It also seemed inhumane of me to let her drown in the ocean of hopelessness with me. Joyce wanted to stay, but I needed to let her go, for her, and that was just what I did.

Sitting with my head on the backrest, heavy with bustling thoughts, I was looking forward to booking the night train home, so I got enough time with my thoughts before I got home to a nagging mom.

I was lost in thoughts that I missed the buzz at the door, maybe once or twice, but when I jerked forward, a rather tall and well-built man was standing in front of me with his arms folded across his chest.

"What the heck? How did you get in here?" I ask, rousing noisily from my seat, with my hand already on my phone, ready to call 911.

"Whoa! Whoa! I knocked a couple of times, but I got no reply. The door was open, so I walked in." He defended, then raised his hands in defense, "I could go back and knock if you want me to." He added, waltzing over to the door before he completed his statement.

He knocked on the door of my office again, which was kind of hilarious, then brisked in with a solemn look on his face. He was huge and looked like a bouncer with a bald head and a husky voice. I took some time to analyze him. He appeared to be in his mid-thirties, probably six feet nine; from his looks, he could either be a bouncer or a ridiculously rich dude.

"Good morning, Doctor Nina." He said, stressing my name. "That's you, right?"

"How did you get in?" I say, completely dismissing what he just asked.

"Through the door? It wasn't locked."

"Who wants to know?" I ask.

"My name's Sekoni, and I'm here on behalf of my boss, who would like to offer you a job as his son's physician." Wait, a damn minute. What is even happening? I didn't know who this man was or how he even found me, but I decided to play along to get some insights.

I looked up from the table, a bit surprised.

"That's very kind of your boss, but I'm not sure why he would need a personal physician for his son."

"I'm afraid the situation is quite delicate," Sekoni continued. "My boss's son was recently involved in an accident, just a fall down the staircase though, but the accident had affected parts of his brain, resulting in amnesia. He's currently being cared for at their estate, and his father is hoping you could help him... medically."

"Your boss, I assume, has no name, or does he?"

"Of course he does," he responds with his brows confused.

"You just never mentioned him, and I was hoping you would've led with that, especially since he could be my potential employer." I respond sarcastically.

"My bad. His name's Will." Sekoni replies.

I looked thoughtfully at him, considering the offer. I didn't even know his boss, "That's quite a unique situation, and I appreciate Mr. Will for believing in me and what I have to offer, but he barely even knows me or what I could do for him." I said, stating the obvious. "I'm not sure if I'm the right person for the job."

"Actually, Will isn't most certain if you are either, but we've heard so much about you. Well, most precisely from the recent research you published regarding children's memory and cognition; he read about it in the papers." *Well, now I know where he knows me from...*

"So, he's trying out every Doctor in Philadelphia?"

"That isn't the case."

"Then, what is?" I asked sternly.

"You need to understand the situation here. My boss is desperate and needs to know which medicine will be quite effective and which will act faster than the others."

"There can't be two masters in the jungle; he has to choose his regret."

"Then, I'm sure he chose you."

Moments whooshed off, but I still had nothing to say. I was stuck in the rut and needed the money, but I didn't want to appear desperate. On top of that, managing a patient isn't just for the money; it's equally to make an impact, and that was what I was about. Probably why I'd gone bankrupt, if I'm being honest.

"I appreciate the offer, and Mr. Will seems very generous. If he thinks I'm the right person for this job, then I think so too."

"It's a deal then," Sekoni said, stretching out his hand for a handshake. His hands covered mine, and for a split second, I felt small.

"Here are the terms of the contract. And one more thing." He said, turning to me, his stare fierce. "Mr. Wills would love to keep this transaction a secret from the public to avoid scrutiny. Letting someone else in on this is a breach of the contract, which could have you sued. I hope you understand?" He says, in his intimidating voice.

Taking the contract from his hand, I flipped the pages, my eyes quickly settling on the salary, along with the benefits, and it was…let's just say my entire lifestyle would change in a good way. I swallowed hard, then look up at Sekoni, praying he didn't notice the greed in my eyes.

"Of course, I understand."

"Good. You start tomorrow. Venue and time of the

meeting will be communicated to you shortly." He said, with an air of professionalism.

"What? What about my clinic? I thought we were using this space?" I say, staring at the space in my office.

"I'm afraid not. Mr. Will wants this to remain discrete, so having us park here all the time will raise brows." He explained.

"Sure," I replied, holding the contract to him.

He didn't say anything. He only nodded, bowed, and started heading out the door.

I saw him to the door, and let him get in his car and drive off before rushing back to take a closer look at the contract. The money was enough to clear off my debts and pay for Mom's medication.

I didn't know who the hell Will was, but I thought he must be a rich man if he was willing to stake such a ridiculous sum of money for his boy, but then, I would do the same for my mom.

Grabbing my bag, I rushed off to my car and ignite the engine, thoughts of booking the train home that night disappearing out of my head. It was top secret, but Mom had to hear about it.

∽

MOM WASN'T in her usual spot when I trudged home; neither was she in the kitchen, her second usual spot after the living room. *That was weird.* She was always perched on the sofa in the living room, waiting for my return to taunt me.

"Mom?" I screeched, barging from one door to the other, eager to share the news with her. I scanned her room, and a glance provided an answer.

I dashed to the living room, and there she was, with her back to the door, her bags neatly arranged. Is she leaving? I thought as anxiety ran through me.

"What's happening? Where are you going?"

She managed a weak smile, and walked forward to where I stood, then placed her hand on my face, "Nina, don't be this way. I have no choice but to leave, and you know it. Don't make this harder than it should be."

"I'm sorry... I just don't want you to go. You're all I have." I spurted, sniffling. Although mom and I have had our moments, she is still my mom and we only ever had each other.

"Baby, I know. But I have to do what's best for both of us. You can't pay your rent, and I've been living off you like a leech. I don't want to do that anymore. I have to be supportive; you know?"

"You don't need to. I got a new job today." I cried.

She paused and gave me a serious face. "No way."

"I'm serious," I said laughing, as tears poured down my face. "Some rich man, I don't know, never seen him before. He offered me a job to take care of his boy. He's going to pay me solid money. We're going to have money soon, and I'm going to pay off the house and clinic rent, I promise." I was talking fast now, wiping my tears with the back of my hand, and laughing almost simultaneously.

"But what about your job?" Mom asked. "You've been looking for a way to get back on your feet; how are you going to do that?" She added, patting my shoulders lightly.

"That's the thing. I'm going to be making more money, so that means I can get back on my feet soon."

"Tell me all about it." She said after a while, and I told her everything... except about the terms of the contract.

4

Will

From my seat, I could hear the sound of water splashing into a glass, another disturbing sign of boredom or an omen of what was to come. The air conditioner was on full blast, but I could still feel sweat dripping down my back.

We were sitting in a conference room in Santa Monica Hotel in Fishtown with the Director of AJ Entertainment.

I adjusted for the twentieth time, absently flipping through the pages of my new plot. I'd taken Margaret's advice; I was going to keep writing; for her mom and for the rest of my fans, who had the best intentions for me.

I was trying in vain to avert asking my secretary to fix me a drink, but then wishing was like telepathy. I didn't need to say it, Lily knew me like the back of her hand. It was fucking scary at times.

"Here." She offered, placing a glass of mild whiskey in

front of me. I smiled at her disappearing frame, grateful for her in my life...in more ways than one that was for sure.

"Are you suggesting we put the publication on hold?" I asked, straightening as Jake's last sentence lingered. Jake was the General Editor at AJ Entertainment, and I'd seen tons of his work, and they were good.

"No, no. Don't get me wrong, but I can feel it in my bones that this is going to be one hit of a book that's going to take Philadelphia by storm. However, I want you to reconsider the offer; slamming the door against this opportunity could be turning your back on one big privilege." He explained.

"You want my humble opinion, Will? I think you should know by now that you won't be in the public's face forever. Grab every opportunity you can lay your hands on with both hands." Says Jimmy, his assistant.

"And don't get us wrong, we know you're already a nutcracker of a writer, and I know it would be rude of us to paint this picture as if we're doing you a favor. But think about this, letting us perform your story in theaters would be a fascinating thing. You could be the twenty-first-century William Shakespeare, who knows?" Ian added, persuasively.

"May I remind you of the extravagant sum involved here? It could last a lifetime." Jimmy said, handing me the contract. I glanced at it briefly, then raised my face again to Jimmy, and for a minute, I regretted not bringing Lily along to the meeting.

"It says here I would get an insurance policy, and I needed to attach which account the money should be paid into." I read out loud. "Do I need a separate insurance policy for this? I have a handful already."

"It's no big deal. It's just a company dogma; you can choose to skip it." Jimmy explained, gesticulating.

"I shall then." I say, calmly.

"We will, however, need the account for the payment and your next of kin." Still, Jimmy, directing me to the part in the contract where I needed to input the information.

I thought hard about it, and when I was convinced that it was going to be an incredible opportunity, I nodded at the men with a firm smile.

Everything was going well, and I was getting into the flow of the conversation. Then, suddenly, I felt like I was in a fog, I couldn't focus anymore, and my mind was wandering. It was like I was in another world, and I couldn't find my way back.

The more I tried to focus, the harder it became. I was getting increasingly frustrated, and started to feel like I was losing control. It didn't take long before I couldn't even remember where I was. I looked around, and I saw that I was in a hotel conference room, but I couldn't remember what city I was in or which hotel I was at. I stared between each man present in the room, completely lost.

I was in a state of déjà vu— I knew I'd been there before, but what I couldn't recall was how I used to navigate back. I felt completely lost.

Just as I was about to spiral into full-blown panic, I heard Lily's voice. "Are you okay?" She asked, taking a few strides to where I was seated. I looked at her, and for a moment, I didn't recognize her.

Each person in the room took turns to ask about my well-being. "Is everything okay, Will?"

Even in my hazy mind, I thought I heard Lily offer a consoling explanation, and sat beside me on the table, signing some papers, while I sat helpless.

Slowly, it felt like a light bulb went off in my head, and I remembered who I was and where I was. "I... I think I was having a panic attack," I said to the men to avoid arousing suspicion.

Lily stared at me, concern apparent on her face. "Can I get you anything? Water?"

"No, thank you." I replied, struggling to steady myself. It felt like I was levitating, and my fingers were trembling like I had Parkinson's or some shit.

"We can stop the meeting if you want. Why don't we go outside and get some fresh air?" Jimmy began to speak in a calm, reassuring voice.

I nodded and stood up, with Lily assisting me to my feet. The three men followed us out of the conference room and into the hallway. I could feel my heart pounding in my chest, and I was having trouble catching my breath.

It took ages for my breath to return, as did my memory, and like a mind reader, Lily knew I'd returned. I couldn't blame her. She'd stayed with me long enough that she could decipher how long I would be gone for and how I acted when I gained my footing again. No kidding, I owed a lot to her for putting up with me, for letting me put her through so much trouble. Ever since my boy fell sick, I had been dealing with severe anxiety to the point where slightest of new settings, which could possibly lead to change or uncertainty, triggers a panic attack within me. I guess this was my way of coping.

"We should go." She said, motioning to the exit.

"I agree." I replied, allowing her to lead me towards the door, like a chaperone, with the three men following.

"Are you sure you don't need us?" I heard Jake ask as I lowered myself into the car.

"Not really. Mr. Will just needs some rest for now," says my assistant to the men.

"Right. Keep in touch; we wouldn't want to hear some

traumatizing stories, do we?" Ian chimed in, and I saw the suspicious look on his face as he glared at Lily, his eyes not leaving hers for a brief second. Lily wasn't one to be intimidated; she gave me a big stare, then a scoff before sliding into the car next to Sekoni. With that, we took off.

I rested my head on the backrest and closed my eyes, fighting back the feeling of helplessness that surged through me. Blacking out was bad enough, but the recurrent incidence of going blank in public and the fact that it was becoming more frequent was getting to me in more ways than I thought.

Fighting back the tears in my eyes, I felt like I was seeing my life fade in front of me, and I was just thirty-four. I wasn't as fucked up as my son, Freddy, and I guess that was where I lost it. He was just a boy and wasn't deserving of the darkness in the world. *If only I could write him a better script, then I would give him a better life.*

I tried to focus my mind on the meeting again, but I kept drifting back to the experience I had just had. I recalled the first time I was diagnosed with amnesia; that was just after Lily officially became my assistant. Right after the first episode in my office, Lily had noticed that I wasn't as engaged as before and asked if I'd wanted to reschedule. I'd agreed, and we'd decided to meet again the next day. I'd left my office that day feeling dazed and confused, and I knew something was wrong. On the way home, I realized that I couldn't remember my address, or even what city I was in. I was lost, and thinking about my son living that way killed me.

∼

Our short trip to East Girard was quite eventful, and the Doctor was a handful. I perceived she was trouble from the moment we throttled into the hospital. She'd greeted Sekoni with an air of familiarity but had greeted Lily and I indifferently.

"Dr. Nina, this is Mr. Will. You'll be taking care of his son, as we discussed yesterday."

"Nice to finally meet you, Mr. Will. Sekoni told me about your son. I'm sorry." She said with empathy.

"What exactly did Sekoni tell you?" I ask, my face bearing no expression of my emotion. She looked from Sekoni to my face. Was she looking at him for approval? *What did they really talk about yesterday?*

"Lily, Sekoni, could you two please give the doctor and I some time alone?" I instructed with my eyes still on the doctor, and the duo obliged.

"Please sit." She'd offered, perching on the other seat, and looking expectantly at me.

"I hear you're good at what you do."

"Depends on who told you that, but yes, I suppose?" She says, with an American accent. She was...shorter than I expected, perhaps somewhere around four feet twelve, with brunette hair and olive eyes. She was quite honestly attractive even in her simplicity.

"I can write a book about you from what I know," I say with a smirk. I'm good with words, can you blame me?

"That's insightful; looks like you've been keeping your ears on the ground." She replied, canceling out my claims.

"I'm sure you've gone through the terms of our contract, Doctor Nina?" I ask, diverting the conversation.

"I sure have." She replies quickly.

"So, will you have any issues with the clauses?"

"You won't have to worry about having my lips tight

sealed. I barely even know anything about you. Sekoni refused to say a word."

"Good. Looks like you and I won't have issues there. However, it's Freddy you'll be in proximity with every day, and I don't need to remind you that my boy is very special. Please take good care of him."

"I promise." She says, raising her hand up in a salute. She seemed unperturbed by my presence, probably because she had no idea who I was, and it was fine that way. The fewer people who know about Freddy and me, the safer our secrets.

5

My heart dipped right down to my chest as I watched the little boy sitting across from me. He wasn't looking at me, and for the briefest second, I wondered if he was ever going to give me a chance to help.

Freddy needs me as much as I need him. As my mind continued to travel and the past few months flickered over and again, I felt my fist clenching.

Get a hold of yourself, Nina.

I took in a deep breath and adjusted on the comfortable, leather couch. The house was exquisite, in , and the furniture was straight out of some upscale décor magazine. A sudden memory brushed through me— one that was unpleasant, enough for my stomach to turn. Damn, I really need to stop my mind from going wild.

Releasing a long breath, I straightened and raised my gaze to the boy's face again. A small smile danced across my lips, and my heart finally began to settle.

"So, what do you want to do today?" I ask, playfully.

His small shoulders shifted in a shrug. "I don't know.

Dad told me to listen to you, so whatever you want." He gives me the widest of smiles. This kid was honestly really precious, and I'm not a huge kid's person.

The smile on my lips broadened. "He did?"

The boy nodded gingerly, but I could see his shoulders relaxing. *That's a good sign.* First meetings are usually tough and uneventful...at least in my experience.

"I was hoping you could tell me about your favorite things to do, perhaps show me as well."

His face scrunched into what I presumed to be confusion. "Really?"

I beamed. "Of course!"

As he ran off and disappeared down the hallway, I peered more closely at the stack of papers before me. It was just heaps of paperwork about Fred; his previous medical record, his routines, and everything I needed to be aware of as we worked together. I conducted a test a few days ago, and I was aware of how severe his condition was. The neurological assessment took longer than I presumed, but the result finally arrived last night. I picked it up and skimmed my eyes over the words that are going to be stamped in my mind for a long time. I was yet to prepare to put together a schedule. I just needed to study Freddy for some time. You know, get to know him before assessing him mentally and emotionally.

"Here! This is my favorite game." Freddy said with delight and hope dripping from his voice.

In his right hand is an iPad, and the other is cradling a truck. I chuckled lightly as he dropped the items in the space in front of me.

"I don't remember the last time I played a video game. I've been so busy being old that I don't remember anything. Maybe you can teach me, mhmm," I say, playfully.

I held his gaze as the question lingered. Outside, I could hear a dog barking and the sound of a car driving down the road. However, nothing overshadowed the loud thud echoing in my chest.

"Take your time. I really want to know how long you've been playing and how good you are." I added. It took all my willpower to not reach out a hand and ruffle his hair. He looked so much like his father – the arrogant man that almost blew my head off with his snappy attitude just a few days prior.

I picked up the iPad and tapped the screen lightly with a finger as Freddy stared at me. I could feel his eyes on me but did not attempt to raise my head.

"I started playing yesterday." He finally muttered. There's something in his voice that nagged at me. Confusion? Disbelief? His eyes were fixed on me, "You still want to play?"

I patted the space beside me. "Come on! Show me what you got!" A smile overtakes his face, "What kind of games do you like?"

I was taken aback by his question, quickly averting my gaze. "Um, I didn't really play games when I was your age. I, uh, spent my time reading lots of books."

"Oh."

Something in his voice alerted me that there was more – that he was holding back something. I waited patiently, hoping he'd open up. He didn't, instead, he grabbed the iPad and proceeded to thumb the screen excitedly. I paid close attention to every movement he made, mentally noting down how relaxed he was and how he seemed to pause in between pushing the characters on the screen.

"I don't know anything about video games," I said as he glanced up at me.

"Here. I'll show you." His expression turned eager as I grabbed the iPad from his tiny hands.

"That's me, and the character in blue is my opponent, Aaron."

"So, we have to kill Aaron?"

He giggled. "No! We are racing against him."

I watched with fascination as he and Aaron fought on the deserted lane. I've seen kids do this a few times, and I always wondered what it was like to be in control. When Freddy grabbed my forefinger and slid it across the screen, making sure I stayed on the right track, I let out a sigh. *He deserved better than to be sick like this.*

In the blink of an eye, I was ahead of Aaron; my speed increased as I pushed forward. Freddy jumped on the couch and clapped his hand.

"You catch on so fast."

I swallowed and tossed him a warm smile. "You're a good teacher, and this is fun!"

"I started yesterday. You can be good too if you keep it up." I give out another shrug. "Do you want to play another one?"

I paused the game and motioned for him to move closer. At this point, it was almost noon. We had spent the entire morning just opening up and playing games, and I quite honestly enjoyed every second. Just then, I noticed the garden outside and decided that we could change things up a bit. We could go for a walk while I ask him some more questions about his life and his favorite pastimes.

"Hey!"

We both glanced up at the sound of the voice.

"Hello." I flashed the woman a smile...Lily. Or at least that's what I heard her go by. "We were just getting to know each other."

In her hand was a tray. She looked surprised to see me, and I wonder if Will didn't inform her of my arrival. She opened her mouth but closed it immediately and made a turn, heading towards a table on the other end of the room.

"I had no idea you were coming this morning. I thought your sessions were in the evening." She tilted her head to the side to glance at me.

"It's Friday. I figured I should get an early start so I can have the rest of the day to prepare for the weekend." I cocked my head. "Is this a bad time?"

She laughs. It's humorless. I've worked with a lot of folks to know when someone isn't straight with me. "It's okay. As long as Will is okay with your decision, then I'm cool with it." What the fuck? I don't know, there was just something off about this chick. It was like she was trying so hard to be on Will's 'good' side.

I look beside me, and Freddy was still immersed in his game. I stared at him briefly. He seemed to have crawled into a shell. Something wasn't right. Just at that instant, I drifted my eyes back to the blonde and almost fell off the couch when I saw her dumping some white substance into one of the glasses. I marked the design on it and swiftly pulled away.

"So, uh, is everything okay?"

I stared right into her eyes. Was *it okay to ask her what was happening?*

"As I said, we're trying to get to know each other. This is our first meeting, and it's not appropriate to dump the procedures on him. I need to figure out what he likes, and I must ascertain the right path to take when treating him. Most importantly, I need him to be comfortable around me."

She chuckled. "He's just a kid. Just tell him what you want, and he'll be right on it."

No shit!

"He's a kid, yes, but he's in a bad place right now, and I must treat him with care."

She gave a nonchalant shrug and then dropped the tray on the table. I moved to snatch off the glass I saw her messing with, but she was quick. As Freddy's fingers curled around it, my chest tightened. What was she feeding him with?

"So, do you like it here?"

I frown. "I do. I love my job, and Freddy is a good kid."

She ruffled Freddy's hair. "That, he is."

I tried to smile, but it wobbled. The air was getting uncomfortable, and I needed her to leave so I could check what was in the glass she offered Freddy.

I busied myself with a file and tipped my head backward. "We must get back to the game. Freddy was just about to introduce me to Aaron," I add with a convincing smile.

She raised her brows. "Who is Aaron?"

Without wasting a second, I nudged Freddy and gestured at him to tell Lily about Aaron.

"Aaron is my opponent in Mario Kart. We race against each other and -"

"Oh, sounds interesting!" She interjected with faux excitement then she stood up. "I must run now. I have a few things I need to take care of before 4 pm." She pinned her eyes on me. "Macho, the bodyguard is right outside the door. Call him if you need anything, and when you're ready to leave, please drop a message."

"Alright." *I can't wait for her fake ass to leave.*

I watch her walk away before turning to Freddy. He was still playing, his bottom lip captured between his teeth. He looked so peaceful. No one had made mention of his mom, and I didn't dare to ask. That piece of information wasn't necessary...*or was it?* Maybe, I will find out someday soon.

I stared through the window as Lily's car pulled away. A few minutes later, I rummaged in my handbag for something I could wrap Freddy's glass with.

"I have to make a quick run to my office. Will you excuse me for a few minutes, Freddy?"

He blinked. "Yup."

I arranged the files and tucked them into my handbag, then dropped the glass gently in the bag too. Dr. Nick should be able to figure out what was in it.

Soon, I was heading towards the hospital on Sixth Avenue, which was only a ten-minute drive away. I mean, I couldn't keep Freddy alone for too long, or else his father would be...not very pleased, but I just had to know what Lily was lacing his food with.

While I thought I'd be in and out within no time, it was a fucking Friday and I lived in the city, so this was going to take longer than anticipated. There were several cars in the parking lot and people moving around. I walked briskly to Nick's office, someone who I knew from medical school, who later went on to be a lab technician; I just knew he could do something to help. When I walked in, he was discharging a patient. I apologized and handed the glass to him, recounting what I witnessed to him.

"You think she's... drugging him?"

"I don't know what to think, Nick. But I can tell you there was something off about her."

He peered at the glass and then motioned at me to excuse him. "Make yourself comfortable, Nina."

I hissed in a deep breath. I knew I just met Freddy, and there was no reason to suspect a woman that had been in his life for much longer. But I just had to be certain she was not harming him in any way.

Seconds ticked into minutes, then an hour. By the time Nick came back into his office, I was at the edge of my seat.

"I don't know how to say this, Nina. You're right to suspect her, and I'm glad you decided to come to me because something seems off."

"I want to assume she has no idea what she's doing."

Nick shrugged. "If that will put your mind at ease, go right ahead. I'll conduct other tests and put you through the results."

Still stunned at Nick's words, I drove back to Will's condo. I had no idea how I was going to tell him about this. *Do I even tell him?* Nick was skeptical of her involvement, but needed to be for certain before confirming, but why would she? My mind jumped to millions of places at once in hopes for finding her true intentions, but I just couldn't imagine the cost of her plan...Freddy.

I pulled into the long driveway; at the same moment, a tall figure emerged from the front doors of the house. It was Will, and he looked pissed. I grabbed my bag and stepped out of the car. *God bless my soul.*

"You better have a good excuse for leaving my son alone." He barked, glaring at me.

His tone irked me. Even though he had every right to be mad at me, that wasn't the way to go about it. He was paying me to treat his son, not to be his shadow.

"I stepped out to get something."

"And you didn't think to wait until your hours were over or tell me?"

I gulped. He was five feet away from me and the scent of his cologne wafted strongly into my nose.

"I'm sorry."

"Sorry? Is that supposed to make everything better? What if something had happened to my son? What if he had an episode?"

I scoffed. "Then, we wouldn't be standing here having this conversation. I would have been on the damn floor begging you to let me live."

At this, his nose flared. I wanted to laugh, but that would only infuriate him further, so I did the only logical thing that crawled to mind.

"Freddy is probably waiting for me. I'm sorry I left without informing you. It won't happen again."

He opened his mouth, but I was already walking past him.

When I reached the double glass doors, I turned back to glance at him. He was right where I left him, his fist still tightly clenched.

Fuck!

6

A host of warm feelings curdle in my belly as I watch the young, attractive women throw her head back and laugh at something my son was blabbing about.

The more I observed them, the deeper my feelings of appreciation became. I knew it had only been a week, but the bond forming between them was unmistakable. Maybe I was being quick to judge, but every time I hired a medical specialist for Freddy, they just seemed to be harsh and impatient. But Nina...she was nothing like that. She took her time with Freddy, she wanted to know him for who he was.

I remembered the first time she met Freddy. He was super excited and couldn't stop talking about her afterward. If I had any doubt about her expertise, it disappeared the instant he recounted the things they did together. The game, the long walk in the garden, and the short stories she told him—it all meant something to him and, by that account, something to me.

Suddenly, it became clear that this wasn't mere attraction but something I'd have to tame or risk getting burned. I marched over to them, keeping my gaze on my son's face.

"Here to gloat, aren't you?" Nina said, tilting her head to face me slightly. I saw a challenge in her eyes and humor. She was silently laughing at me, and that grated on my guts.

Does she know about my ailment?

Just when I opened my mouth to shoot back a retort, she flashed me a winsome grin.

"Freddy is incredible. He's doing remarkably well."

I allowed myself to relax at this. "It's all you. He talks nonstop about you during dinner and every chance he gets."

Her brows quivered, "He does? I thought he'd be too preoccupied with his video games and schoolwork."

For a moment, our gaze locked, and then she swiped her tongue over her bottom lip. My belly tightened, and something warm fluttered down there. Immediately, I shifted my gaze to my son as he knelt on the floor to pick up whatever rolled from his table.

"Hey, buddy!"

Freddy smiled and crossed the floor, rushing straight into my open arms as I squatted on the floor. "Dad!"

"I see you're having a great time. How was today?"

He glanced up at Nina, then back at me. I could see the struggle in his eyes, but there was strength too.

"It was good. I made an airplane."

I tousled his hair. "Can I see it?"

Without saying a word, he sprinted out of the study; his footsteps echoed on the marble tiles.

Moments later, he returned, clutching a sketchbook.

"Here!" He opened a page, pointing excitedly at a drawing that looked more like a bicycle than an airplane.

"Oh buddy! This is the most beautiful plane design I have ever seen. Good job," I replied.

I watched a dozen emotions flash across Nina's face. There was pride and adoration. And she exhibited a determination that was akin to my little boy. It eased my mind to know that my son was with someone who genuinely cared about him.

"He's going to be alright." Her words tinged with undisguised hope.

ONLY UPON ENTERING my bedroom did my breathing return to its usual pace. As I unbuttoned my shirt, I struggled against the images of Nina running her dainty and perfectly trimmed fingers across my hair, her lips seeking mine in a nerve-wracking kiss. Each nibble, each teasing touch brings me closer to a release that's only portrayed in one's imagination.

"Fuck!" I growled, clasping my fist into a ball, urging my racing heart to quiet down and alleviate the discomfort in my pants. Nina's beauty was incomparable. I've met quite a lot of women, and none had dared to rouse so many emotions in me within a short period. I guess it had a lot to do with her soft, nurturing side. It stirred something within me.

For most ladies, they always have to try a lot harder – going the extra mile to please me. But not her. She's effortlessly made her way right into my thoughts, clouding my mind with her laugh, smile, and thoughtful gestures towards my son. For the briefest instant, I was curious about the idea of being enveloped in her positive aura and reveling in the brilliance that emanated from the core of her being.

Another groan slipped past my parted lip as I dragged my underwear slowly over my shaft. It was achingly aware of the thought buzzing in my mind. The intensity of my attraction to a woman I've only just encountered was beyond what I could have imagined, even though we shared no common ground...well, apart from my son.

Somehow, I found myself under the bone-chilling sprays, running my bathing sponge over my heated skin.

Stop thinking about her!

I sighed, placing my palms on the bathroom wall so the water ran down my bare back. As the water rinsed my body, I tried to focus my mind on something else. *Think of...I don't know...fuck—maybe a teapot?* By the time I stepped out of the shower, my body was calmed, and I was more in control of my breathing.

An hour later, my bedroom door slammed open, and Freddy walked in with his iPad tucked under his arm. A smile stretched across his face when he spotted me, though his eyes appeared distant. He got into my bed and snuggled against me; his arms wrapped around my midriff.

"Do you wanna play a game?" I asked when he said nothing for a long minute.

He shook his head. "I just want to sleep for a bit." He said, then closed his eyes.

Soon, gentle snores escaped his mouth, and his hold loosened.

That night, as I lay in the dark, replaying the last few hours and imagining how the next few weeks would be, I shivered with dread as the thought of forgetting the most important aspects of my son's life hit me repeatedly. Freddy is worthy of the utmost care and attention, and I'm ready to go to extreme lengths to provide just that.

Despite my effort to keep my distance from my son's doctor, her images persisted in occupying my thoughts. Her beautiful eyes, her voice, her sarcasm, her floral yet fruity perfume lingered in the house for days, even after she had left for the day. It was just everything about this woman that had me in a trance.

On Friday morning, I came home after a meeting only to meet her alone in the study. *What was she doing there? Where was Freddy?* I turned on my heels, but her voice pulled me to an abrupt stop.

"You know, my first day here, I was scared shitless. I needed this to work so badly, but then, I had no idea what to do." She dived right in, without any foreword.

I leaned on the door, watching her intently. "Why were you scared? You were highly recommended, and your reviews were quite impressive if I'm being honest. Does that happen often?"

"Not really." She frowned.

"Well, you didn't make it any easier. You practically lashed out at me on my first day."

"I'm sorry," I said quietly. "I thought you had left Freddy alone, and I didn't know how to react. You know how much he means to me."

"Do you mean how to react or how to tame your anger?"

I closed the distance between me and the table to where she was, fiddling with Freddy's toys.

"Both?" I made a feeble effort at a wisecrack.

She chuckled. I stopped at the edge of the desk and shuffled through the pile of papers.

I used to work here most nights. However, since Nina started, I've moved my stuff to the basement, and set up a temporary office there.

Her gaze dropped to the paper in my hand. "That's Freddy's profile. I like to document everything."

My interest was piqued, not just by her brilliance but by seeing how she glowed under the bright bulbs – gorgeous in a dark blue pantsuit that brought out the glint in her eyes. I had no idea what I was doing here. I planned to stop for a brief second, inquire about Freddy's progress, and ask her if she could take on another--

"Looks like you have something on your mind. What is it?" She says as she cuts my train of thought short.

My eyes bored into hers, warmth dampening logicality. "I just want to hear you talk about work...I mean about Freddy."

"Oh. Everything you need to know about me is in my resume. I sent a copy to your email. As for your son, I already told you how well he is doing. He will make a great comeback; I am sure of it!" She says with such excitement that I couldn't help but smile.

She adds. "I know. You probably don't trust my judgment."

"I've seen you with Freddy a few times, and I must admit you are doing a terrific job. I'm beginning to nurture this hope that he'll be fine. So yes, I trust you, Nina."

She straightened, stretching her arms on the desk. My eyes shifted to her fingers. *Fuck!*

"Okay..." She muttered with a low chuckle. "Do I make you uncomfortable?"

"No." I gulped. Did something give it away already? I perched on the edge of the desk, close enough that my leg could brush hers if I moved an inch. I didn't know what the hell was going on right there – or since the moment I met her. I wanted to tell her about my fears, about my dreams, my nightmares, the ugliest parts of it all, and I wanted to watch her try to soothe me – talk to me like she did with Freddy.

Was that wrong? Am I crossing a line here?

She was watching me intently, her brows furrowing. I

adjusted, and my leg rubbed lightly against hers. She stiffened but made no move to pull away.

"Are you really here to talk about your son, Will?"

I breathed out slowly. "No. Uh, yes." This woman was making me fucking nervous, and I've never even been nervous around women before.

I waited for her to say something, maybe even push for more, but she sat still, watching me from the corners of her eyes.

"Wine?" I asked, pulling away from the desk. She was making me want to throw caution to the wind and take her right here on the desk.

"I-um...I don't think that's appropriate."

I returned her stare. Just a couple minutes earlier, I received a call from Lily that Freddy was at the park with Sekoni, so my best guess is that Nina was here to catch up on all the paperwork. "Freddy isn't coming back; besides, I'm your boss. I won't hold it against you. You know?"

"I don't--" She attempts to speak, but I cut her short.

"I have something to tell you, and I need you to drink with me while I share, so it doesn't seem awkward or anything," I said with deliberate smoothness. I've concluded that I could trust this woman. My voice dropped to a murmur, "Is that alright?"

Her eyes melted into a gleam. "I guess so."

I managed to make it to the bar at the other end of the room and poured some of the amber liquid into two wine glasses. I walked back to her, my lips curling in a charming smile. When I handed her the glass, she took a small sip, then closed her eyes, her brows knotting in concentration.

"Marsala?"

I grinned. "Indeed. It's one of my favorites."

We sat in silence for a few moments, sipping from our

glasses. The atmosphere was relaxed and comfortable. But shortly after, I broke the silence by heaving a long sigh.

"Freddy isn't the only one, Nina. Sometimes, I wonder if it's my fault that he's that way. I don't know why I'm telling you this or if it even matters, but I get scared when I ponder on everything that's going on."

A lump formed in my throat. "Right now, it's partial, but I'm concerned it might worsen over time."

"I'm sorry." She said with a blank stare.

I waited, expecting her to say more. She must have noticed because the edges of her lips quivered in a small smile.

"Freddy's condition isn't your fault, Will. While he's your son, he's on his journey. In fact, his own, unique journey. Don't be too hard on yourself because, honestly, you're doing a terrific job with him. But um...as for yourself, if you don't mind me asking, of course, is everything alright? She asks in a hushed tone.

"Yes. I have a doctor actually. I was in rehabilitation for two months, then she suggested we try cognitive therapy."

"How's that going?"

I shrugged. "Not bad. I can remember what I had for breakfast today so that's a good sign," I say with a chuckle. Nina was one of the most recognized specialists on cognitive therapy in the city, so talking to her about this felt absolutely fitting, but I didn't want to simply get her sympathy.

She grinned. "That's great! I'm hopeful you'll be fine, Will."

"Don't do that." I echoed.

She shot me a puzzled stare. "Do what?" Her voice was laced with humor.

I felt more at ease. I dropped my glass and allowed my finger to slip into my pockets as the need to touch her increased. She was so beautiful, and her smile was so pure, so enchanting.

"Nothing," I replied.

The sun was already setting, and the hope I'd been nursing was taking on a larger shape.

"Will."

Nina's voice was soft yet soothing. I tilted my head to face her, my gaze hard on her lips. I was aching to see her reaction and figure out if the heat buzzing around was one-sided or if she could feel it too. She lowered her gaze and bit her bottom lip. When she raised her head, her expression was masked, and her eyes gave nothing away. *Am I imagining things?* Fuck, I didn't even know if this woman had a boyfriend or even husband. I should've had one of my assistants investigate that, but I never imagined to be wanting to make a move this quick.

"If you need any help or have anything you need to share, please don't hesitate to reach out to me." *Fuck me. There goes everything I imagined out the window.*

I wanted to ask her if I could kiss her and feel her skin against my fingers. I wanted to ask her what crawled through her mind when she gazed at me, but those are just...questions that I probably would never get to ask for the sake of Freddy.

"Goodnight, Will. I will see you on Monday." She says with a warm smile, sipping down the last of the wine and making her way out the study room.

7

"You've got to be shitting me, Nick." I spurted, unable to conceal the grievance.

My fingers were trembling as I took another superficial look at the report in my hand, redirecting my eyes to where I wanted it to go like I was controlling a cursor. The sheer amount of substance, more specially, drugs, in the kid's blood was abnormal. Was Lily behind this? But why? *That cunning little bitch.*

She'd been a part of Will's family for decades—even before the birth of Freddy—and according to Will, she was the best aide.

If he was so confident in her, why would she dump portions of ketamine in Freddy's drink? I was starting to doubt whether she was the mastermind behind Will's amnesia, too.

Nick had slouched back in his seat and was watching me with keen interest from where he sat.

"You look rather annoyed for someone who had suspected she might be playing Will for a fool."

"I don't know, but I guess I'd actually thought I could

give her the benefit of the doubt, you know? I was hoping the results would prove me wrong, but this... this is just proving how right I was!"

"As expected, Nina. Now, the real question is, why?" Nick adds, trying to understand the situation.

I shrugged, "I can't even wrap my fingers around it." I replied, and we sat in silence for a while as the clock kept ticking from seconds into minutes."

"What are you going to do?" Nick asked, after a while.

"To be quite honest with you, I don't know," I replied, letting out the air that had filled my air sac from the shock and horror.

"You can't tell Will. No, not yet. I mean, you just started working with him; he would think you're trying to break the family apart." Nick says after thinking through the variables at hand.

"No, I know I can't. He doesn't even know me, so he wouldn't believe me. It could be my word against hers, and I can't put myself in that kind of situation. I'm there for the money, so I should stick to the plan and not go around poking my head around when I shouldn't."

"And the boy?" Nick asked, and I found myself encapsulated in a river of pity. My mind flew back to the puny and fragile creature I went to treat every day, and my heart sank.

The little boy didn't deserve any of this; he was just a child. Freddy always seemed so far away, so scared and vulnerable when he blacked out. Why would anyone still want to hurt such a delicate soul? He couldn't even hurt a fly.

Thinking about it there, it made sense – father and son are both amnesiacs. What didn't make sense, despite how much I tried to figure out, was *why?*

"You know, Will is amnesiac too?" I revealed, and Nick spared me a 'shut the fuck up' look.

"You'd better say you were kidding." He said, wide-eyed.

"I'm not; I wish I was, though," I replied, tilting my head.

"In this case, we have where to point fingers at." He answered, adjusting in his seat.

"But we have no evidence."

"You saw it; you could testify." He says, as if stating the obvious.

"That's not enough," I argued, then took another deep breath. "No one's going to believe me. You have to remember that Lily has been part of the family for a long time, so rather than just run away in circles, I think we should prescribe some drugs to restore homeostasis."

"You do that, you're closer to the boy." He adds.

"Yeah, I did that already. I've written some Doctor's notes, and I'll get the medications at your pharmacy before I leave." I said, rising to leave.

"Nina?" Nick calls out to me as I reach the door. I cocked my head around to someone who looked deep in thought.

"What?" I ask.

"Try to be discreet. You might be swimming in dangerous waters here," Nick advised, and I felt the hairs on the surface of my skin arise.

"Thank you," I replied, nodding. "I'll be in touch soon," I say and shut the door behind me.

∼

I COULD TELL Will was in the facility the moment I drove in through the barbed wire gate, and my mind danced around to the last time I ran out without informing him. Strangely enough, I just knew deep in my heart that he wouldn't flare up if he got to know why I was out that day.

Strolling in with my gut in my hand, I kept rehearsing the words of my affirmation, imagining his reaction, and praying that he would hear me out before calling me all sorts of crazy. I dropped my bag on the table and picked up my stethoscope, unsure as to why I needed it. *Maybe to seem even more professional?*

The consultation room was empty, and so was Freddy's playroom. There was no sign of Freddy, nor his father, which was strange because I'd seen Will's car outside.

"Will?" I called out, suddenly feeling a familiar scent filling my nostrils. However, there was no sound, and for a brief second, I thought I felt the silence cast a suspenseful theme in the room that got me scared. Just then, a hand grabbed me from behind and pushed me against the wall. *Will.*

"Oh my gosh! You scared me!" I exclaimed, breathing heavily as I brought my hand to my chest, hoping to soothe my beating heart. In response, Will brought his hand to my face, tangling a strand of my hair with his finger. His eyes were on me, yet they seemed so far.

"Do you need anything?" I ask, wondering how much of the poison he'd gulped down today and seeing in his eyes the fate of a man surrounded by thorns and foes rather than friends.

"Where have you been, Lily?" He asked, his voice low, throaty, and slightly aroused.

Lily? My mind repeated, wondering what other relationship Will had with her aside from work.

"I'm...I'm not Lily," I mumbled, wriggling to escape his grip, but his hand continued tracing down the slope on my back, finally settling to my sculpted ass.

Will cupped them with his hands, massaging them and lifting me closer to meet his height. Even with his pants on, I could feel his arousal, and unconsciously, it aroused me.

"I-I should go," I muttered.

"No. Stay. I need you." He begged, planting a kiss on my cheeks, then another, and then another.

I knew he had no idea who I was at this moment, so how would he know who he needed? To him, I was Lily, and I felt wronged. It felt like I was taking advantage of him, or maybe even vice versa. Covering the tiny space between us, his hands shifted from my ass, then ran over my torso and found my boobs. Slowly, he unbuttoned my bra and fondled my nipples, while his other hand slipped in through my panties and began massaging my folds.

"Oh my...God!" I exclaimed, shocked at my body's response to a man I barely even knew, and seconds later, we were both engrossed in deep kisses. I couldn't recall the last time I'd had sex with a man. With being so mentally out of it because of my debt, and my mom's constant taunts, I just never felt sexually aroused. It felt like I was being celibate, but I couldn't hold it in anymore as I drew him to me, wrapping my left leg around his hip, paving room for his fingers as they found my tight pussy. I moaned harder as the movement of his fingers inside me transmitted an impulse right through my skin, filling my pores with serotonin.

He planted a kiss on my lips, and I responded, astonished by how gentle his lips felt on mine and how his fingers did the opposite...in a magical way. Moments later, our lips were in fierce combat—each of us fighting to win. Then slowly, his lips dropped to my neck, sucking on the skin, then moving to my tender nipple. He suckled on my right tit, his finger still performing the upthrust and down thrust motion that blew me away. He was just so fucking good with his fingers. *I wonder what else he is good with,* my mind wandered off.

My hands ruffled his hair, throwing my head backward as the sensation built. Standing, he plucked off my clothes, tossing them on the floor alongside his. As he buried his face in my cleavage, he dragged a perky knob into his mouth and suckled on it, lifting me from the floor. I could feel his hardened shaft as it felt ready to be buried deep inside me, and a groan escaped his lip.

I curled my toes, each thrusting in and out, causing a sporadic spasm as he rocked his hips nonchalantly.

"Fuck!" I squeaked, watching between hooded gazes as my tits hung out, flopping around with each thrust.

"Oh, you feel so damn good." Will moaned beneath his breath. Bringing his face to my neck, he locked the back of my neck, holding my head in place with his elbow.

A grin sat on the lines of my lip as the sensation ratcheted up, a signal that I may experience orgasm for the first time in a very long time.

"M-more!" I caught myself saying, then felt a finger on my tit. He squeezed it roughly, nibbling on my shoulder blade simultaneously. It felt so good as ecstasy blurred up any feelings of caution that remained. I buckled my hips slightly and spread my thighs wide apart to give him more room to thrust into me even harder. I gulped in the air as he hit harder, brushing on my sweet spot, and then withdrawing. *What was he doing? Was he avoiding a climax?* I thought as my fingers clawed on the wall aggressively.

In response, I heard him let out an almost animalistic growl, so I knew for certain that he was enjoying this as much as I was. I widened again as he pulled out slowly, almost driving me nuts. With a knee-jerking thrust, he plunged in again, causing me to shift slightly from the wall as I raised my hips to him.

"Oh...yes, fuck!" I gagged, moving my hips to the rhythm of his movement as he rocked and jammed into me like a wild beast throttling in the mainland.

Soon, we were on the table, back to the wall, and then on the floor, with him still romping in as hard as can be. It felt like hours had gone by, and we were at it at every position on every piece of furniture one can possibly make love on.

After all was done, we both lay wasted on the hard floor, and as I stirred to look at his face, my heart sank. He was sleeping peacefully, like he had no worries, and in my heart, I knew he might never remember this moment, but I would. I would live with the memory of being used by a man who blacked out and mistook me for another woman. I couldn't even label it as rape, it was consensual to some degree, and I won't deny it because I enjoyed every second of it.

For a brief second, the feeling of disgust and self-pity replaced the feeling of ecstasy that had warmed my heart initially. I felt insulted and used, but neither surpassed the feeling of pity I felt for both father and son.

As quiet as can be, I picked up my clothes that were scattered in different positions across the bedroom floor. I made sure to place a blanket over his bare body, so he wouldn't feel cold in the cool December night of New York. Of course, I was aware of my disheveled hair, so I brushed it with the back with my hand, palming my face and resisting the urge to bend over again. I couldn't deny it; the sex was good, and I wanted more.

Would I ever learn to look Will in the face again after today? I mused as I stuttered to my car.

I was going to possibly resign soon. I mean, I couldn't

dare to look into his eyes anymore—not after what transpired between us. I thought that was the best decision at the time until Freddy's image flashed before my eyes, and I realized that I'd created a bond with the little boy.

The resolution to stay for Freddy's sake swallowed the shame of banging his dad.

For Freddy, I heard my heart whisper, and I slumped into my car, still tormented by what was to come.

8

I still recall the feeling of confusion that had engulfed my mind when I woke up on the cold floor completely naked. After adjusting to the brightness that shined from the window, I make my way to the bathroom to get refreshed for the day. Today just felt different. The walk downstairs felt a bit...strange. Maybe it was because I had no clue about what happened last night.

The cold wind brushed against my skin, and I smiled as pieces of last night started to come to me. It was difficult to recollect when my memories had returned, but I recalled feeling buried deep in pleasure, the energy and passion involved. It was unlike any other moment from my past, and I have been with a fair share of women if I am being honest.

I had no idea when this mystery woman left, but I hoped that I didn't do the wrong thing by her. Zoning out could be difficult sometimes, and aside from Lily's mean jokes about how animated I get each time I fuck her when I'm out, I know I could be kind of rough. But...Nina wasn't Lily, which was why I was scared. I didn't want to hurt or disrespect her in any way, especially not after the way she took care of Freddy.

Rousing from the window, I paced down the length of my library, which was one of the largest rooms in the condo. The shelves were made of clean, white lacquer, with hidden lighting that illuminated each book. There were flower vases placed at each edge, just the way I'd dreamt my library would be as a child. It was a safe haven for me. Each shelf had a label and contained first editions and rare journals, encyclopedias, and some obscure leather-bound volumes and fine art prints that are quite hard to find elsewhere. The décor was kept to a minimal since I often used this place to write ideas for my books and didn't want the décor interfering with my imagination; I wanted the room to serve as a blank canvas, if that makes any sense. However, I did have a small garden, and a waterfall, providing a calming oasis in the middle of the library. It was just perfect.

There was a part of the library I kept out of bounds, though. It was where I hid my collections of obscene books, poems, and art. Not that it made sense why I hid them. Everyone's got some dirt in their mind, but I had them hidden because they were my private collections for erotic scenes.

There was an open floor, with plenty of glass walls and high ceilings, giving it this spacious and airy feel, and the best part? There was a window close to my garden, which I looked out to when I had writer's block, which wasn't often. Everything in my library was meticulously thought through because it was the best place for me to spend my days.

Even Freddy loved it there. He used to play hide and seek, hiding behind flower vases and shelves as a child, but all he did now was read books. He was slowly growing into an introvert, or perhaps it was just the ailment that had sequestered him from the rest of the world.

Standing by the large table in my library, I took the last gulp of the amaretto that Lily had dropped for me, enjoying the crisp liquor that ran down my system. It felt exhilarating, and then my phone beeped. *Sekoni.*

"Talk to me," I said, and immediately I answered the call.

"I just arrived at the facility." He replied.

"How's my son?"

"As happy as can be," Sekoni replied in his unusually dry tone.

"Okay then. I will see you soon," I said and ended the call.

I dunked the rim on the table, and drove to East Girard with thoughts of Nina stalking me. It was unnecessary to go to the facility, but I wanted to see her face.

I couldn't defend the thoughts of her breaching through my mind. It was like she'd captured my soul and cast a spell on me.

Maybe I should pursue her? Like officially ask her on a date. But the other part of my mind instantly tells me it's too soon.

Don't people say when a man knows, he knows? I knew what I felt, and despite being a little different from what I write in books, I knew there was something between us.

When I saw her perfect figure at the door, I knew I could never stop thinking about her. There was just something strangely different about the way she styled her brunette hair that morning, but when she waved at me. It was indifferent; perhaps it was just me expecting her to feel the goosebumps, as did I.

For the rest of the day, I thought she was trying hard to avoid any form of contact with me, but I was determined not to let her have that. After her session with Freddy, I slipped my arms around her wrist, holding it firmly yet delicately as she tried to break free.

"Are you intentionally avoiding me?" I asked, realizing she hadn't even looked at me the entire day.

"What if I was?" She responds very calmly. *What the heck?*

"I could roll over if you did," I replied, and that seemed to work as she raised her face to me.

Something in those eyes made me want to swirl her behind the door and fuck her, but that was inappropriate, but my cock suggested otherwise. Her reaction brought a smile to my face. I was freaking out, conscious of my beating heart and the flurry her gaze brought to my eyes. I was infatuated by a woman who could handle a man like me, a man with too much going on, and her playing hard to get made it worth it. It made me want to win her over.

"So, what's this about?" I asked, pretending I couldn't see through her.

"You tell me?" She said challengingly, folding her arms around her body, still giving me a cold shoulder.

I dipped my hands in my pockets and shifted on my feet, enjoying the diplomatic banter. I opened my mouth to speak but kept silent unintentionally. I don't know what she'd done to me, but the Nina effect was unbreakable.

"What do you want to hear? That I like you?" I asked, feeling the heat of my body rise. She lowered her eyes briefly as if retreating, but when she looked up again, they had a different type of fire in them.

"Is that supposed to make me giddy?"

"Depends," I answered, matching her fire.

She covered the space between us, tugging at my chest with her finger. "You think you like me because you had sex with me, and we both know that wasn't intentional; you'd only done that because you thought I was her." She said fiercely, her tone defiant.

I cowered, and my countenance dropped. What the actual fuck?

"Nina... I am so sorry." I pleaded, reaching out to hold her, but she swatted my hands off and paced away.

Judging by her flushed face and angry expression, I could tell she was hurt.

"I'm sorry, Nina. I promise it wasn't intentional; I would never take advantage of you."

"Thank you for being honest." She replied, and I realized that I'd just hit myself on the head.

"I-I didn't mean it that way." I can't believe I was stuttering.

"What do you mean, Will?" She asked, saying my name with so much authority.

"I didn't mean to take advantage of you or the situation."

"But you did, so please don't insult me like that." She said, anger visible in her tone.

I couldn't let her leave in this state, so I lunged forward and stood in front of her, blocking her from getting to the door.

"Just hear me out, please." I pleaded.

She said nothing except throw her face to the window, with her chin high. I shifted uncomfortably, realizing how long it had been since I last fought with a woman.

"I promise, I had no idea what I was doing." I started swallowing the gulps that were forming in my throat from the nervousness. What if I lost her? What would happen to Freddy...he was finally starting to make progress in years.

"Yes, I admit it wasn't intentional at first, but everything changed after that day. I can't tell when I started feeling this way, but I know how I feel about you, and I'm certain that I care about you." I said, feeling energized again.

"I...I think I am starting to fall for you, Nina," I repeated, searching her eyes for answers, but they said nothing. Her olive orbs only searched mine as if reaching down my soul to uncover my motives.

"I don't know, Will. This isn't real; this cannot be. You're my boss, and I want to maintain things and remain professional." She responds, completely ignoring my confession and I won't lie and say that it didn't hurt me and my ego.

"Who said we can't work things out?" I asked, covering the space between us. She inched backward, and I forward, like a predator reveling in the fear of his prey.

"Can't you see why?" She asked, worry lines creasing her face.

"I can't see anything wrong with this, Nina. I know I am into you, and I would be the happiest man if I knew you felt the same way."

"How can you lie this way to me?" She teased, throwing me a light punch.

"If you can't see through me, how could you tell when I lie?" I said, my eyes blaring the fire of my need.

"Not to generalize, but don't men do this? Lie to get what they want?" She asked, spreading her arms. *Oh...who hurt this poor woman? Who made her want to lose all hope in love altogether?*

"I don't know about other men, but I'm not them. Give it a chance." I say with the sincerest smile

She let out a smile, then looked outside. I noticed her face flush a deep pink and the longing in her dreamy eyes when they fell on me again.

Taking the initiative, I move a step forward and wrap my arms around her, pressing her into a deep kiss. We both stood tall, brushing our lips on each other for a while, saying so much yet saying nothing. As I lowered my tongue into her mouth, I heard her sigh incoherently; then, a short moan escaped her, which only turned me on further.

"Does this mean what I think?" I asked after she broke the kiss.

"Depends on what you're thinking." She replied, laughing, and curling the corner of her lips. I resisted the impulses my body sent to grab her for another kiss.

"So, what do you think about us?" I say, clearly hinting at her thoughts about our kiss moments earlier. I have never wanted to be validated by a woman, but this just felt different. She was different in every which way.

"It...was really good, honestly." She responds with her head lowered, and I could tell that the once daring woman was now blushing.

I take this as an opportunity to ask her a question that had been on my mind since I laid eyes on her. "Would you consider giving us a chance?" With that, she simply nods and I hold her in a tight embrace.

"But I do have one question you must answer before this could even go further." She says firmly.

She took my silence as her cue to ask. "Why me?" Instantly, I knew what to tell her, but I didn't know what to start with. "Nina...you're different...and in a good way. You are caring beyond words. You go out of your way to care for Freddy, which is something I never saw with other woman, whether they were my partners or a one-night stand that happened to see Freddy on their way out. Besides that, you have humor that I can appreciate, you are playful, beautiful, energetic. I don't fucking know, you are special, Nina." I say in a single breath and sigh at the end.

Wasting no time, she follows up with another question, "Do you want me that bad?"

"I do."

"How badly?" She asked, playfully.

"So bad." I replied, wrapping my arms around her waist.

9

That morning was like every other morning, but there was something exceptional about it that made it different. I was going to see *my* man. It just had a nice ring to it. It felt nice to finally have my life on track, with someone I appreciated.

The thought filled me with so much energy but made me equally anxious.

Will wasn't a stranger; we saw each other every day and, despite how quick we were moving, I couldn't wait for the next time I got to see him.

With that, I begin to get ready for work. I lined my lips with a red lip gloss and caked my face with finishing powder to ensure my makeup was set for the entire day. I embellished my ear with two gorgeous silver earrings and smiled at my reflection in the mirror. *I hope he likes what he sees.*

"You've never been so enthusiastic about dressing up for work, Nina. What's changed?" Claire, who had been watching me like a mom inspecting her teenage daughter, asked. She had been my housemate after I moved near Will's condo to make sure I was on time for work. I wasn't going to lose this job, so I made sure to do everything in my power to stay even if that meant moving places. My mom, on the other hand, stayed back at our old place. I still owed rent, after all.

"What's wrong with looking a little unconventional?" I asked as I cocked my head around to meet her eyes, still fixing my face.

"I don't know." She said, shrugging. "Perhaps it's just the amount of time and effort you're putting into trying to look this way. Who is he?" She says, almost knowing that this was all for a man.

"Claire...I don't." I start but she cuts me off.

"You don't what? I'm just curious. When your friend acts strange out of the blue, you start to wonder, don't you? Wouldn't you notice if I started to dress differently one fine day?" She says with a raised brow.

Rolling my eyes, I swirled to face her, "I'm seeing...uh, someone," I was going to tell her but remained silent because I knew Claire would scream out her lungs, awakening the entire neighbors on the second floor.

"I can sense something off about this. Now, I am even more invested. Nina, you know you can trust me." She said, giving me a pitiful face. I hesitated for a while, then dragged her to the cushion and perched beside her to tell her everything that had been going on in my life for the past couple of months.

"So, I told you about the little boy, Freddy, right?"

"Wait, please don't tell me you're involved with the kid. I would never forgive you." Claire cut in, alarmed, rightfully so.

"No, what? Let me finish!"

"I'm sorry, Nina." She begged. "I won't cut in anymore;

just tell me, please." She promised, with her hand up, as if imitating an oath.

I had to think long and hard this time, "You won't make me feel like a creep this time?" I asked, with an attitude.

"I promise." She replied, with her hand still up.

"Fine," I said, rolling onto the cushion again. I could tell she was itching for the news.

"Okay, so Will, Freddy's father, asked me out the other day at work. It was completely unexpected. Heck, I didn't even think he saw me like that, you know, I'm just some Doctor who cared for his son. That was all I was supposed to be." I whispered, conscious of my searing inferiority complex.

"Oh, Nina. You talk like a twelve-year-old. You're everything in one, and I thought you'd grown past this." She said, cupping my face in her hands. "You make yourself a doctor; the profession didn't make you, and no more talks about being less beautiful because you are the most beautiful woman I've ever seen." Claire continued.

"You know, you sound like Will right about now," I said, and we burst out laughing. Sometimes I enjoyed her company...keyword, *sometimes*.

"Aww! Tell me about the horrifying things both of you have done behind closed doors." She says with a mischievous grin.

"That is for another time," I replied, making a stand.

"Why?"

"Because it's a bad idea. You can't shut your mouth."

"What? I promise it's going to die between us." She said, zipping her lips with her hands.

I should have seen through her to know that it was such a bad idea, but no, I decided to give her the benefit of the doubt.

Biting my lips, I allowed a naughty smile to escape the corners of my upper lip; then I crouched next to her again on the cushion. Here we go again...

"Well, not so horrifying, but I think my ex-boyfriends could learn a thing or two from Will." I say and wink at her.

"Is he *that* good?" She asked, eagerly.

"Absolutely. He kissed me so passionately, and then we had sex for hours."

"Oh my! This is so exciting!" Claire screamed in shock, then covered her mouth after realizing how loud she was.

"Shh, keep it down." I hushed, putting a finger to her lip.

"I have to go, now; I'm running late," I said, running out, slamming the door, and letting out a deep breath, glad I could escape.

"We'll continue this conversation when you return." She said through the window as I was out the door already.

"Oh crap!" I heaved, running to my car. If I could cure Freddy and Will, then maybe I could give the case of the old man in the mansion a try.

∾

I TOOK a moment to brush off the disheveled strands of my hair before gazing at the tiny mirror of the car again. I could feel my pulse and rising temperature, but I didn't care much about it; I was going to see him. I guess the thought of that kind of blurred out every other fear.

I made an entrance, feeling my anticipation rise. However, this time, someone was standing in the reception area in front of me, but it wasn't him. It wasn't Lily, neither was it Sekoni.

When she turned, I was able to clearly take in her features and, if anything, she looked like a real-life barbie doll. She was blonde, fully adorned with accessories that caught me wondering how much they cost. Her hair was perfectly trimmed, and her clothes looked like they cost about three months' worth of my rent money.

"Hello." I started, and she smiled, exposing her perfect teeth.

"Hello, Nina." She replied and I was, obviously, taken aback. *Who was she and how did she know my name?*

"Surprised that I know your name?" She said with a wave of her hand, looking away.

"It's only natural that I know the name of the woman fucking my man behind my back." She spat the words like venom.

I stuttered, my heart lurched violently, and my stomach tightened as I struggled to stand on my feet.

"Let me guess, he didn't tell you?" She asked, scoffing. "It's a shame. He only wanted to have a taste of you. It's what men do, and last I checked, Will is like every other man, my darling." She said, making a pitiful face. I was just stood there...completely speechless.

"Natasha?" Will's voice sounded through the door, and we both tilted our heads in the direction of his voice. Just then, Freddy's voice drowned Will's as the little boy raced to hug the woman in front of me. Was this Freddy's mom? Were they married? A million of questions suddenly flooded my mind.

"See what I mean?" She asked, raising her eyebrows, almost sounding surprised. I didn't understand until later. Natasha bent over, wrapping Freddy in a tight hug that lasted for eternity.

"Take the child away." I heard Will command, and Lily hurried to comply, leaving us three in the room. Natasha strolled seductively towards Will, swaying her hands and carrying herself with pride.

"Hello, darling." She greeted with grace and charm.

"What are you doing here?" Will asked, interjecting her salute. His eyes flew to me, and I thought I saw him soften for a second before showing disgust when looking at Natasha.

"Nina and I were just talking about you not telling her about me. Such a shame you kept us a secret." She said with a pout.

"I didn't keep anything a secret; we just do not exist anymore, and that's the truth," Will replied, holding her gaze, and I could swear that I saw defeat smeared over Natasha's face, but she appeared to be an incredible actress.

"Fine then. Let's say we're nothing to each other, but what about Freddy? He's the one thing you and I have in common." I knew it. She *is* his mother!

"Freddy is our child and that is it. We can love and care for him independently." Will says.

"If that's the case, I want custody of my son, Will."

I heard Will scoff and the muscles of his face clench, "You can't have him. Are you insane? You dumped the little boy when he needed you the most... when he needed his mother. We both know you do not care about him."

"And you do? Do you think you care more about my son than I do? I'm his mom, and no one loves my baby like I do." I felt so lost in between hearing both parents fight over their child.

"If that's true, then your actions speak differently," Will answered, ending the argument momentarily.

"I'm going to have my son back, Will," Natasha said with a soft yet formidable voice.

"You seem to have forgotten something, Natasha." Will

started, looking like he was in control. "The Pennsylvania law defines abandonment as a parent's willful failure to perform parental duties for at least six months, and how long have you been away from the kid? Three months? Five years? Maybe six?" With that, he walked off, leaving her limbs weak and her breathing intensifying with rage.

"Will Nicholas Declan," Natasha yelled at the top of her voice. "I'll get back at you. I'll take everything you have, and I'll make sure no one will be there for you at the end!"

Natasha turned to me, her eyes blazing with anger. "What?" She squeaked.

"You're Will Declan?" I asked, looking at Will, and in a flash, Natasha transmogrified.

Smiling, she sidled close to me, with her hands on her hips, she asked, "You didn't know?" She scoffed; glad she'd found a sore to feast on. "I wonder what else he's keeping from you. Will is such a secretive brat."

"Natasha!" Will yelled, growing from angry to aggravated.

Natasha smirked, then turning towards the door, she stopped, "You'll meet my lawyer soon, Will."

"And I would love to watch you twist your ways through the law," Will replied.

"Oh, that can be arranged; laws are meant to be broken." She smiled, and winked at me, leaving the door ajar without even bothering to shut it.

She left Will and I alone, and for a while, we stayed in silence. In my case, I was rather to hurt to think of anything to say, though I couldn't speak for Will. In my heart, I knew that Will was still a stranger, and except when he began to talk, he would forever remain a stranger.

10

The moment I saw Natasha at the door, I knew the foundation I'd struggled to lay with Nina was going down the drain. In my defense, I just didn't want to make her uncomfortable; there's this creepy feeling knowing about who you're working for does to you psychologically, and I didn't want that. She had mistaken me for someone else, which was the initial intention, but everything had changed from that day.

"Nina," I whispered, taking a step forward, and I watched her take a step backward. I won't lie, that really stung more than I thought.

"When were you going to tell me?" She asked. I was afraid she was going to cry; and that would be heartwrenching. "Let me guess, you weren't going to tell me, were you? Did I even mean anything to you, Will?"

"Nina." I started again. It felt like my vocal cord was tightened, and my brain was freezing from cognitive overload. "I swear, I was going to tell you everything. I just wasn't sure when; I guess I was just looking forward to the perfect time, and I ended by fucking things up."

"Yes, you did. You screwed up big." She said. "Do you know how it makes me feel hearing this from someone else?"

"I can imagine," I replied.

"No, Will. You can't imagine. Gosh, I feel like a home-wrecker. Did you hear what she told me after I entered? 'It's only natural that I know the name of the woman fucking my man behind my back.'" She repeated, biting her lower lip in embarrassment. "She thinks I'm having sex with you, I'm not a whore, Will, and it was just once. Who did you tell?"

"No one," I replied.

"That's impossible." She spat. "I know that men kiss and tell, but I'd thought you'd be different."

"I told no one, damn it!" I knew I was being honest, so how had Natasha known about the facility and Nina? It was glaring, these walls had ears, and they could talk too, but there were no pointing fingers.

Nina let out a shaky breath, then waltzed off with me behind.

"What do you want from me?" She yelled. That was where I lost it.

"You're only mad at me right now, but you won't sign me out of your life entirely, will you?" I asked, feeling like a child.

Even in her rage, I could tell that those words suppressed her anger for a while, enough to allow her to think logically.

With a sniffle, she wiped her eyes with her hands and exhaled again.

"We're still working together; we have a contract, remember? Plus, I'm doing this for Freddy." She said and walked off again, leaving me alone with my thoughts and my body shaking violently.

A glance at my trembling fingers was enough proof that blacking out was imminent. I stuttered, lost my footing, clutching my stomach as nausea built, almost ripening. My sight became blurry, and I could barely make out the objects in the room. Yet, in my hazy state, I thought I heard Freddy scream excitedly as he ran from his room to the patio before stopping in his tracks. It was like I was in my house, and Freddy was an even younger version of himself. I thought I'd seen that scene before as I stretched, searching my attic for recognition, but nothing clicked.

He was looking at something. No, someone. It was a woman who'd broken a vase by accident, I presume, and hidden the flowers inside another vase. She put her hand to her lips, warning him to zip his mouth. I stretched further; then, my vision went blurry.

A screeching sound punctuated my vision, as a car revved to a stop, and someone burst into the house, visibly pissed. They gulped down something in a glass that appeared to make their stomach churn. The screeching sound continued, and soon, I was holding my ears, breathing through my mouth as streaks of sweat broke on my forehead. My forearm grew weak, as did my limp, and jerked to the floor, unable to stand.

"Dad." I heard Freddy cry, accompanied by Sekoni...after this, everything turned black.

∽

THE STENCH of antiseptic flooded my nostrils as I stirred, struggling to rouse yet held down by the anesthetic effect.

In my fatigued state, I heard the faint sound of an ambulance blaring in the distance, returning to the hospital with some casualties while I pushed through the crowd, hoping for a safe place to relinquish my rage. That was when Natasha was being a thorn in the ass.

I'd dashed into the house and met Lily in my library, arranging the books. I hadn't assigned her that task, but I was too unsteady to think properly. Again, she'd dropped a glass of whiskey on the table and left a note for me to drink it, in hopes that I would feel better and calm my nerves.

Walking to the table, I dragged the glass and emptied the contents into my mouth. The drink left a strange taste in my tongue, which I'd attributed to the substance Lily had dumped into the glass before pouring the liquor. Must be a dream, I thought, shaking the image off, but it wouldn't leave. What the fuck? I'd seen her dump some strange substance in the glass yet, I hadn't confronted her? I was puzzled, but still asleep, then I heard Freddy screech, and I followed the sound of his voice.

It was the same vision I'd seen moments before blacking out, but it had looked more vivid this time, like it was part of me, but something wasn't the same as with the first vision. In the second vision, the woman didn't break the vase and hid the flowers; she'd broken it on someone's head and was searching for something. I saw her put her hand to her lips when Freddy appeared. At the same time, there was a man, in a pool of blood, which looked incredibly real. The woman had apparently broken the vase on the man's head possibly killing him---when I tried to zero in on that man...it appeared to be Grandpa Declan.

Immediately, I yelled, but I felt dizzy like I was swimming in a whirlwind; then I blacked out too, but I had been awake enough to make out the face of the woman who'd killed my grandfather. It was Natasha, but there was someone else; her image was fuzzy, but I knew her name.

My eyes flew open, and as I rolled to my side, hers was

the face I saw as I jerked back to consciousness. She smiled pleasantly.

That was neither a trance nor a dream; it was... real. I could feel it in my fucking bones. *Lily...what have you done?*

∽

IT HAD BEEN two days since I got discharged from the hospital, yet I was still unable to wrap my head around how I felt after regaining part of my memory. I reached my hand to touch the portrait of my grandfather on my table but drew my hand away. Nothing had changed, yet everything seemed different. I recollected my conversation with Dr. Trevor right after my first blackout, and lines fell into place.

"There's a region in your brain called the amygdala that's been frozen; you must have hit your medial temporal hard." Doctor Trevor explained, displaying the video of the damaged part of my brain on a monitor.

"I don't understand. Does the amygdala freeze when you hit your head or when you take in drugs that could possibly knock you out?" I asked, slightly confused. If he was the one prescribing my drugs, then he was invariably the one causing some issues.

They'd all been working together, I thought as I sat in my library anticipating the events.

"It's her," Sekoni informed me.

"Follow her," I commanded, and I heard him step out of the car and into the crossroad.

"There's a car here whose plates look familiar."

"Read it out."

Sekoni did, and it didn't take long to decipher who it belonged to.

"Looks like Natasha," Sekoni confirmed my suspicion

after a while. There was a long silence for a while; then, I heard him take to his heels, racing for his car as I heard from the other end of the line.

"What's happening?" I inquire, wanting more insights.

"Natasha offered her something."

"That's it. That is what she has been using all along." I said out loud. "Thank you, Sekoni, I knew I could trust you," I said. At that point, it was difficult to decide who was on my side and who wasn't. I knew I couldn't trust anyone, and that filled me with as much rage as it filled me with sorrow. I could survive this, but was my son bait for them?

Fuck! It made sense now. I was right about one thing—my amnesia had only begun after Lily began working for me. Not just that, but so did grandfather's death, and my son's illness, but why? Nina must have known about the drug, I mean, she is a doctor after all and did tests on Freddy pretty often, but why hadn't she informed me?

After that day, one thing was sure...Lily hadn't been lending any helping hand. She'd only been the alchemy with the deadly portion, and Nina was right; my medication wasn't healing me; it was killing me. If I must survive, I had to play smart and pretend I was still suffering from amnesia to uncover the truth entirely.

11

Nina

"There's someone at the door." Mom yelled at the top of her lungs.

It was nearly impossible to silence the sound of his voice in my head, and I swear I'd heard him repeat that sentence a million times.

Just how long did he need to trust me enough to tell me everything about him? I puzzled as the now familiar gut-wrenching feeling crept in again, and my face flushed.

As restless as I was, I looked up from the heap of books on my desk and glanced out the window at the tiny droplets falling freely to the ground while my mind wandered off. I was totally oblivious to my surroundings.

The chant of the rain was exciting, I thought, as it bounced on the rooftop and rolled down to the soil, but nothing exciting was happening in my life. Everything was at a standstill, and my feelings were numb, well, except for the familiar pang in my chest that left me feeling sick all day.

It'd been three days since I discovered that Will Nicholas was the obscure ninety-year-old amnesiac millionaire who lived just adjacent to my house. Although I'd promised to continue working for him, I just didn't have the nerve to face him.

How on earth do I explain the coincidence? How in the world did I skip that part of asking about where he resided? That one question would have solved a lot, or not, but it would have saved me from looking like a fool in front of Natasha that evil bitch.

I was still mad at him, but more at myself for letting my feelings ruin me.

Just what exactly was I thinking? I thought as I dragged my weight off the seat and throttled to the window. I touched my fingers on the pane like it was some magical object that would come alive at the slightest disturbance, and then a sad sigh escaped my throat as I recalled our intimate moments together. I was swimming in the nostalgic feeling of the days he held me in his arms when I basked in the scent of his strong cologne, and our lips tangled like they were meant for each other. Those were the best moments of my life, and it's a shame that it didn't last.

The rough sound of a dry cough resonated behind me, but I was just too lost in thought to flex a muscle, but shortly after, a soft pat on my shoulder brought my mind swirling back.

"Hey." Mom whispered gently that it sounded like the sound of the wind as it swayed past my ears.

Directing my gaze to hers, I took a moment to study the smile of concern that creased her face, and for the first time in a long time, I felt my energy transferred to someone else.

Mom had been acting differently since the day I returned from the facility. It was like she could sense the shift. I didn't ever want to see her worried. I hated the wrinkles that gathered on her face or the eye bags that suggested she hadn't been sleeping well.

"The doorbell rang, my dear, and I think it's for you." She whispered, but this time, her voice was firm.

I blinked aggressively, but my brain was too dull to respond.

"Should I ask them to leave?" Mom continued, ignoring my confused look.

Shaking myself awake, I took a second to collect my thoughts, and smiled broadly.

"I'll take it. Thank you, Mom." I replied, and she shook her head slowly.

Releasing my shoulder from her grip, I wobbled like a boat on a turbulent sea towards the door, silently praying that whoever was at the door was gone by the time I got there.

My hand on the doorknob was about to turn the lock when I drew back abruptly as my eyes caught sight of the image in the mirror.

I blinked hard, then sidled close to the mirror. *This isn't me.* I thought as I gazed closely at the pale image.

"Oh no," I murmured as I brushed my hand over my hair, tucking the tangled strands perfectly behind my ears and tying my hair into a ponytail. Another glance at the mirror said I looked a lot less homeless, and with that, I moved to the door. As I opened the door, I was faced with my worst nightmare and my jaw dropped.

Donned in a black halter dress that accentuated her perfect curves, with a shimmering red lipstick smeared across her lips, the corners of her mouth twisted cynically, and she swiped her car key across my face.

Without even saying a greeting, she pushed past me into my shared apartment, holding her tasseled designer handbag with just her index finger. Literally, like something straight out of the movies.

"How did you find me?" I asked, as my eyes swept all over her body, conscious of her intimidating appearance, especially the way she swayed her hips.

Natasha scoffed, and a grin tore the corners of her mouth.

"That sounds like a foolish question, don't you agree, Dr. Nina?" She responded, her eyes scanning through every corner of my house. "Considering what we have in common, it was easy to track you." She completed, then shot me a stare, one that suggested she didn't find me a worthy opponent.

"So, this is your place? Not bad for a woman like you." She said, still shooting me the wry look.

"You haven't mentioned why you came," I interjected, folding my arms across my chest.

I watched her eyes drop slowly to the hands folded across my chest. To which, she simply rolls her eyes.

"Listen here, I didn't come to fight you. I came with a proposition." She responded.

"What is it?" I ask, yet I remember to remain cautious because I know how vicious she could be.

"Looks like you and I have something in common." She said, pausing momentarily before picking up her pace, "There's no denying that Will has hurt both of us. Your heartbreak is none of my business, though, but I have an offer for you."

"What's that?" I asked, completely uninterested.

"I'm aware that you're going through some financial crisis and would do with some assistance." She paused, shooting me a sideways stare. "That can be solved, you know?"

"And why would you want to do that for me?" I asked after considering her offer.

"It is a case of woman supporting woman. I just want to help you get a life." She answered calmly. *Wow, thank you,* I think to myself in annoyance.

"Wait," I said, blinking fast and trying to process her last statement. "According to you, you're trying to give me a life?" I asked, focusing my attention on her face as I laid emphasis on the last part of her statement.

I guess she caught my expression, "Nina, I'm not here to battle with you, which obviously can't happen because I can't bring myself as low as on to your level." Gosh...how punchable this woman is. What did Will even see in her?

"Oh yeah?"

"Yes, my sweetheart because I heard it's dirty down there."

"Really now? I bet it's not as dirty as abandoning a four-year-old without even looking back." I attacked.

"Oh, you don't say things you know nothing about." She interrupted rudely, her face flushing a deep red.

"I know nothing about it?" I asked dryly, a humorless smile spreading across my face.

Natasha drew closer to me, "At least I'm not the one Will couldn't trust enough to open up to. You know what else? You can never be fully his. Never." She said matter-of-factly.

I felt my stomach tighten and my face flush as the pang swept off the little speck of pride I had left into the trash. That felt like a slap across the face, and I felt streams of tears flood my eyes, but I wasn't going to give her the satisfaction of seeing me defeated. I felt even more angry that Will had kept me in the dark about his identity; resentment washed over me, twisting my core.

"Have you finished?" I inquired, still holding her gaze.

There was a moment of silence between us, during which I brisked to the door, trying hard to keep my stride steady so I don't give my emotions away. Placing my hand on the knob, I swirled to look deep into those brown eyes, holding my breath and raising an eyebrow, I whispered, "You should use the door, Natasha."

She let out a dry laugh. "Misery thrives in the dark."

Natasha took three strides towards me, just enough so I could see her clearly.

"Look, I know you're delusional, so I'll just clear the air. There will be no future between you and Will, so why not save yourself the trouble? Consider my offer."

"Or?" I asked defiantly.

"You wouldn't want to find out, my darling," Natasha replied with a scowl.

"What are you going to do to him?" I asked, suddenly aware that Lily may have been her aide all along.

"That does not concern you." She replied with a straight face. "Take the offer and get out of here or stay and find out what it looks like to be on the side of life." She finished, looking out the window.

Suddenly, Natasha seemed like one of those predators I'd read about. There was nothing she couldn't do to keep anyone out of her way.. I wasn't one to be tossed around, but I could tell I would be poking at a stronger force if I tried to wrestle with her.

"Screw your offer," I said suddenly, and Natasha shot me a knowing smile.

"As expected, I won't come here again, Nina. But be

careful and watch your back," she said, focusing her attention on me. "There can never be a future for you and Will. I hope you keep that in mind." She completed and breezed out the door, wearing a victorious smile and leaving me visibly shaken and dizzy.

12

Will

"Look at me, Nina," I called out, yearning for her attention, but she stood unhinged. She wouldn't even look at me.

"I hope you get well soon, Will." She tossed, and I knew that felt like a goodbye.

"Wait. Tell me something," I asked, my voice needy, hoping it would make her stay. "You aren't leaving right? I don't want you to resent me, especially not over this."

"Why does that matter to you?" She hissed, and I felt hypnotized. I never wanted to see her mad or even upset.

"I'm sorry for keeping the truth from you, at that time, I thought I was protecting my son. I would never do anything to hurt you, I promise," I pleaded, tears in my eyes.

"I need to go. I'm sorry." She said, starting to walk towards the door, but stopped abruptly.

"I do have something to ask before we part ways." She

said, forking around to look at me. "Did I mean anything to you?" She asked, her voice laced with sadness that I felt my heart shatter.

You meant so much more than I could say, and you mean everything to me right now, I thought to myself, but the words couldn't form itself.

I watched as disappointment bruised the last shred of hope that was left in her spirit, and without hesitating any further, she swung the door open, "Get well soon, Will, that's the only way to survive."

"How can I even do that when I can't even trust anyone?" I add quickly.

"You'll find a way; I know you will." She said, and that was the last I saw of her.

It had now been days since I last saw Nina but it was a struggle to get my mind off her and on the Attorney that was pacing the courtroom I was currently in.

I shut my eyes and reckoned my mind back to the courtroom. Surprisingly, it obliged.

Once again, the courtroom was quiet after the chaotic stir that had gotten everyone talking at the same time. I watched as Natasha's lawyer walked forward and presented some documents before the Judge.

Although the documents still appeared neat, it was obvious that they'd been messed around with a couple of times.

"My Lord," the prosecutor continued, "My client has offered considerable proof to back up her claims that the assets were transferred to her on the date written on the documents and that she is entitled to everything stated in the documents signed by the accused."

"Objection!" Lawson, my defense Attorney, yelled as if he read my mind and was about to argue that the documents were forged when the court clerk recalled that he was paid, but we hear the gavel. The sound pierced through the room, and in a twinkle of an eye, the courtroom fell silent again.

"Proceed." The Judge motioned to the Plaintiff's lawyer and the man I'd come to recognize as Wesley proceeded, inviting me to appear before the counsel.

It was going to be a tough case, I knew that. I was aware of the possibility that I might lose everything I have, especially considering the fact that those papers were signed with my signature.

I knew that I had the right to avoid interrogation, but what did I have to lose testifying, even though it meant placing myself into Natasha's trap?

I roused from my seat next to my defense Attorney with so much pain and waltzed to the witness stand, just in front of the Judge, with my face to the crowd. I was sworn in, and the interrogation began.

"What's your relationship with the Plaintiff?" Wesley began, and I looked across the room to where Natasha sat, confidence boldly written on her face like she could predict the verdict.

"She's my ex-girlfriend."

"By ex-girlfriend, you mean you both once had an intimate relationship, am I right?"

"I'm afraid so." I replied.

"I'm equally aware that you two have a son together, this is accurate too, correct?"

Where the fuck was this going? I thought, as I nodded in affirmation and then replied, "Affirmative."

"Did you transfer some money from your account on the twenty-seventh of January to Miss Natasha's account?" Wesley asked with some level of conviction.

"There must have been some discrepancies there

because I transferred some money to my son's account, and I have evidence to proof that transaction." I replied, matching his tone.

"What if I show you the original receipt of the transaction?" He offered.

"Let's see what you got." I replied, suddenly feeling uneasy. Tearing my eyes away from his, I redirected my gaze at my lawyer and saw the look of despair in his big blue eyes. To be honest, I'd never seen those receipts because Lily oversaw them, and every time I'd ever carried out any transactions, I'd done so just before having one of my attacks.

Retrieving the documents from the Judge, Wesley presented them before me and resumed his explanation.

"This document is the report of the transaction you performed on the twenty-seventh of January." He said, laying it in front of me. "This," he said, pointing to another receipt, "is the transaction you performed after you completed your contract with Amazon on the fifteenth of February."

I glanced at the documents, unable to lift a finger to touch them because I was scared everyone would see my shakiness. The documents were new to me, but my signature was on them. Wrecking through memory, I tried to recall what happened on those dates.

"I'm sorry, but I'm only seeing this document for the first time." I protested.

"Then why do you have your signature on them, or is this not your signature?" Wesley asked, a wry grin coming alive on his face.

"That would be all." He said after a momentary pause, and I climbed down the witness stand, feeling my bones go numb.

"Next witness, Miss Lily Johnson." Wesley called, and I

thought I felt my chest tighten in betrayal. Lily galloped majestically to the witness stand, took her oath, and sat down.

"Who is Mr. Wills Nicholas to you? Wesley began again.

"He is my boss." She replied.

"Would you say he was a *nice* boss?" Wesley continued, raising an eyebrow at her.

What kind of question was that?

"Miss Lily," Wesley continued with another question, "Tell us everything you know about your boss."

"Mr. Will was an amazing boss, on the outside." She said, shrugging.

"What do you mean by 'on the outside'?" He responds.

Lily shot me a fearful glance, and that was the first time I'd ever seen her look vulnerable.

"Mr. Will has amnesia, and during those moments where he blacked out, he always did molest me." She said, and bursted into tears.

"What the fuck? That's not true!" I protested at the top of my voice, but the noise of the crowd drowned the sound of my voice.

Once again, the courtroom was a cacophony of noise as everyone spoke at the same time, some jeering at me while others shuddered. I saw all of those, but amidst everything, I saw the triumphant smile that sat on Natasha's lips, and I wondered what else the bitch had up her sleeves.

Once again, the gavel collided with the sound block, and everyone went quiet.

Wesley gave her some time to recollect herself before resuming the interrogation.

"How many times did your boss molest you?" He propped.

"As much as he wanted." She said and wept some more,

wiping her nose with the handkerchief Wesley offered. She gave the crowd the pity card they needed, and they all blindly accepted.

Natasha did a great job, and Lily...well, she was a wonderful performer.

And just when I thought I'd gotten enough shocked for the day, Dr. Trevor appeared on the witness stand, and I didn't need anyone to predict the verdict of the case.

Moments later, it was Lawson's turn to lead the interrogation, and as he walked majestically to the center of the courtroom, I said a silent prayer. Lawson carried out the necessary protocols, then Lily appeared at the witness stand.

"And did you try reporting your boss to the authority?" Lawson asked.

"No."

"And why would that be?"

"Because he swore, he was going to kill me." She replied.

"Do you have a witness to this?"

"Yes."

"Who's that?"

"Miss Natasha."

"And I wonder why you didn't inform your family members or friend, but you chose a stranger. May I know your relationship to your witness, please?"

Hah! That was it; that was Lawson's noose on her neck. Lily shot Natasha a brief stare, confirming my doubts. Everything they'd said was planned, and it was obvious they hadn't thought about that. Pacing away from her, Lawson retrieved the Doctor's report from the Judge's table and walked back to the visibly uncomfortable Lily.

"And you said, your boss was amnesiac, right?"

"That's right."

"You know he had amnesia, so why would you let him sign those papers when it's clear that he's about to lose consciousness?" He asks simply.

"It's difficult to tell when he would zone out. You know, one minute he's okay, and the next, he's out."

"That doesn't sound right, Miss Lily." Lawson said, "From the testimony of our witnesses, we gathered that you were the only one who was quite conversant with his case." Lawson said and gave her a cold stare.

"Do you still remember your meeting with the representatives of AJ Entertainment at Santa Monica Hotel, in Fishtown? We have Jimmy and Jake here today, so you might want to have a word with them." Lawson said, shooting her a glance. "These gentlemen provided evidence, Lily, so think again, or I may be forced to present the evidence to this court." Lawson finished, leaving her alone at the witness stand.

I hadn't expected that to have such an effect on her, but the next moment, she was technically begging Lawson against presenting the evidence.

"The thing is..." She stuttered. And the moment Lawson winked at me; I knew he'd achieved the result he wanted.

∽

I COULD HEAR the whispers and murmurs as I walked past everyone else to my Attorney's office, careful to keep my ears on the ground for criticism, not that I cared, though. I was innocent, and it was just a matter of time before we proved our case.

The case had been adjourned to the next two days, and that is more than enough time for Natasha to take everything from me.

I retrieved my phone from my briefcase and dialed Nina's number. I still had no clue where she'd ran away to, not that I couldn't track her, but I needed to respect her privacy. But...I needed her so bad. I knew that her voice alone could make me feel a thousand time better.

However, expected, she didn't pick up. She hadn't been receiving my calls, and I'd sent a dozen messages. I was only hoping she could answer the phone, just this once. Just as my mind was racing to what she could be doing, she answers. With that, I answer with the first thing that came to mind. "I need you," I say with full conviction.

13

Nina

The evening breeze of early summer kissed my sunburned skin, and as the smell of freshly baked bread wafted into my nostrils.

I couldn't recall the last time I stood with my back to the bakery. It was a simple life in Oberlin, and I missed it for all its simplicity.

"Nina!" Claire's dad greeted me as he drove slowly past in his G-wagon, and I waved back at him.

"How's your leg?" I asked.

"Oh, it is getting better." He replied with a thumbs up.

The poor man had been suffering from joint issues for as long as I could remember. Speaking of, that was the crazy thing about my neighborhood— everyone knew everyone, the more reason I had frowned against coming back here. It's just that nothing could remain private here.

I said hello to a few other folks and started past Elm

Street to our house. I was gradually growing impatient and couldn't wait for Mom anymore. Dragging my feet down the dusty road, I stopped in front of the church and looked up at the crucifix. It used to be a beautiful sight as a child, but that wasn't the case that morning; the sight of the man on the cross bearing so much pain brought tears to my eyes, and I knew just why.

A deep whimper escaped my throat as I fought the tears tickling in my eyes.

"Hey." The sound of the voice startled me, but I didn't swirl around. I knew who it was already.

Wrapping her hands into mine, she whispered, "Let's go."

"Yeah." I replied and beamed her a half smile as I allowed myself to be led the way.

It must have been difficult to take up her bags and leave Philadelphia with me without asking questions. I knew that I owed Mom an explanation, and I hoped I could make it up to her for being such a pain in the ass, but when I opened my mouth to speak, there were no words to say.

"Thank you, Mom." I finally said after we'd arrived home. She said nothing, only smiled, and then placed a warm hand around mine.

Mom's new silent behavior wasn't only disturbing, it was slowly becoming an issue for concern. When I'd asked her to leave Philadelphia with me, she had left without objecting, which was kind of weird and so unlike her.

"Mom."

"It's nothing, Nina. You think I have no idea what's happening to you? I'm your mother, my dear."

I was speechless. We hadn't discussed anything about Will, but now, I was wishing that I had confided in her.

She heaved a deep sigh and came to sit next to me.

"Sometimes, life doesn't give us what we ask for, or what we want."

"I never asked for Will."

"But you wanted him after you got to know him, didn't you?" She asked knowingly.

There was no objection to that; I thought as I felt goosebumps crawl out my skin.

"Mind you, my dear, you're not a coward for retreating. Sometimes retreating is just the wisest thing to do, to protect the future and yourself."

"Retreating? How did you know, Mom?" I whispered quietly.

"I'm no kid." She responded with a sharp laugh. "I overheard you talk to your friend, Claire, I know everything. But I wish I would have helped you sooner." She said sadly, and the feeling of helplessness engulfed me like a fog.

"It is not your fault, mom. Besides, we must live in the present like you always say...so, what do I do now?" I asked out of the blue.

Stretching her hand across my chest, she tugged my chest with her index finger, "Follow your heart, sweetheart. That's all there is to do." She whispered.

"Mom...." I called, and just then, my mobile phone wailed, and it took just a glance to know who it was.

Will Nicholas.

I had nothing to say to him, but one quiet stare in Mom's direction said everything.

As corny as it sounded, I took it as I sign that I had just asked for seconds earlier.

"I need you," He said, desperation in his voice.

I heard his muffled breathing, like he was stuck in a pool and was delirious of air.

"Nina, I need you." He repeats, and I feel the butterflies

in my stomach.

Another pause, but this time, I used the moment to savor the sound of his voice. The desperation in his tone, the longing, and the love was heartwarming, yet I had nothing to say to him, absolutely nothing.

"I miss you." He says this time, and for a second, I thought I heard a sniff escape his throat.

"Come back to me." He begged. That was too much to tug at my heartstrings, I thought as I hung up.

Dropping the phone on the table, I brought my hand to my chest and felt the heaviness in my heart. Tears gathered in my eyes, and my fingers trembled violently.

"Why didn't you say anything?" Mom asked from behind, completely taking me aback.

"There was nothing to say." I replied, fighting back the angry river of tears poking inside my eyes.

"Yet you're hurting from unspoken words. Don't you think you'll breath better if you emptied it out?"

"Will lied to me!" I yelled and sprang to my feet.

"But you love him, don't you?" Mom answered, matching my energy. *Love*...that was the first time I heard it being paired with Will, and it made me evaluate how I felt for him instantly. I did have feelings for that man, there was no denying it.

Mom continues, breaking me out of my thoughts, "I'll tell you what... go talk to him, and when you see him, throw tantrums, humiliate him if you have to, but don't fail to let your heart speak afterward. That's the only way you can truly find out if you're in love with him." She said solemnly.

I never knew Mom could give such advice, but in my heart, I knew I had made my decision.

"My Lord, if I may, I have a witness who has new testimonies that this court needs to hear." Lawson announced, and for what seemed like an eternity, the Judge only considered the new development before nodding in affirmation.

"Dr. Nina Ross." Lawson introduced, and everyone's head tilted towards me.

Stepping into the aisle with my gold satin sundress playing around with the wind and all my nerve endings on alert, I was conscious of the sound my heels made as it collided with the floor. I could equally tell that I was the center of attention, and as I watched their faces burn, a smile spread across mine.

Turning to Natasha, I swear I saw rage written all over those big eyes and confusion come alive on her Attorney's face, but I paid zero attention to them. What I didn't do, however, was look in Will's direction, but standing there in the witness stand, I felt his eyes on me. Honestly, it felt like he didn't blink even once; his eyes fixated on every part of me.

"Dr. Nina Ross, can you tell us about your relationship with the accused?"

"Of course. I worked for him as his six-year-old son's personal Doctor."

"And why's that?" Lawson asks.

"That's because the little boy was beginning to show symptoms of amnesia."

"A little boy, how's that possible?"

"Well, you see, he had a ridiculous amount of drugs that have amnesia like symptoms in his system. Although at a percentage less than that of his father, it was still enough to make a boy of his age black out." I respond calmly.

"So, are you suggesting that the boy's amnesia was induced?" Lawson asks again.

"That's right."

"Then... it's possible that Will's amnesia too may have been induced?"

"You got it."

"Wow! That's new." Lawson said, then paced around. "We'd spoken to Will's Doctor, and he never made such revelation. In fact, he said that Will's case had no cure."

"Not when you treat the symptoms, and not the cause," I chime in.

"So, how did you find out that Freddy's case was induced?" Lawson asks, bringing out the question I had been begging to clear since the first day.

That was the point, I thought as I shifted on my feet. "The thing is, I have witnessed Lily carry a substance in her purse. I've seen her couple times dump some of the content in the boy's juice, and I'm afraid she does the same to Will's alcohol." I responded and threw my gaze at Will, and for a moment, I wished I hadn't. Just like before, his eyes were fixed on me. The impassive expression on his face gave me a stomach-tightening feeling as my heart fluttered repeatedly. I blinked hard as I tried in vain to keep my head in the case and ignore the presence of the stunning man in the blue tuxedo whose eyes were wrecking my soul.

"Do you have evidence to back up this claim?" He asked.

"Yes, I do." I said, handing him the report I got from Nick. "And my colleague, Nick, can also testify."

"That won't be necessary. We have all we need here." Lawson interjects, presenting the reports to the Judge. I took that second to steal glances at Will, but I didn't have to because he held my gaze for longer than expected.

Hours later, the hearing was finally over, and our minds

were at rest after the Judge pronounced the verdict. In my opinion, I'd expected things to get heated badly courtesy of Natasha and her team, who seemed like they had a lot of tricks up their sleeves.

I was wondering what would have become of the case if I hadn't brought in the lab results. *Would Will be sentenced to prison for fraud?* But as I walk toward my car, I feel a firm hand grab me from behind.

I gasped as I spun around to see Will behind me. He was so close that I could feel the heat radiating from his body. I could hardly breathe.

"Hey." He started in a hoarse voice I'd missed hearing, his eyes boring into mine with need and hunger.

"Hi." I replied, trying hard to sound steady. "How have things been?" I asked, taking a deep breath as I observed the need in his voice reverberate through my skin and goose-bumps form on my skin.

He didn't reply; he only kept his eyes on me as he stared deep into my eyes. I was so lost in this stare that I didn't see him move, but the next moment, his arms were wrapped tightly around me, and I thought I felt the planet stand still.

The smell of after-shave and his masculine cologne filled my nostrils, and I stopped breathing for a second.

"I've missed you, Nina." He muttered, saying my name like it was some sacred anthem.

"I'll take the key." He said, and I handed it to him without second thoughts.

"And your car?" I asked after I climbed in to sit beside him.

"Sekoni will take care of it." He replied as he climbed into the driver's seat and sped off, stirring up a tumultuous wave of dust into the air.

14

Will

The moment our feet hit my bedroom floor; it was crash landing on me as we wrestled against the ravaging need that stirred within us like a volcano creating a path to erupt. Soon, my tux was lying on the floor, and all I had on were my pants and socks.

Everything happened in record time, as we both lunged at each other like we'd been starved. I dragged her on top of me and pressed into her, making her feel how hard she got me. I struggled to stay in charge while her hands traveled randomly from my face to my neck and to my back. Breaking off from the kiss, my lips made their way down her neck, and I kissed her sunburned cleavage. Whatever had her exposing her skin to the sun, I was going to find out, I thought as she bit down her lips to stifle the moan that lumped in her throat.

Drawing a line on her back, I snatched her from the

ground and held her midair while kissing her with so much need - the need of the past few weeks. I wasn't mad at her, if anything, I was glad she was in my arms again, and I wouldn't let her leave ever again.

As I made my way down her body, to her perfect ass, I lifted the gold satin gown she wore over her waist, giving my hands the liberty of traveling past the barrier of flesh and into her core. Burying my face in her chest, I kissed her everywhere, and felt myself getting even harder.

The button on her gown fell off, exposing two round and perfect breasts. I'd seen them before, but they were just as exciting to enjoy as the first time. I thought as I lifted one into my mouth while my hands toyed with the other, and the moan she'd been trying to stifle came undone.

"Fuck!" I heard Nina moan in a hushed voice, and I grinned.

Wait for it, I thought, and with that, I drove my finger right into her whilst I continued suckling on her boobs. Nina hiked her knees and threw her head back while her hips wriggled in my arms.

"Oh my...gosh!" She screamed loudly. *Good thing Freddy was busy with Sekoni.*

However, that was accompanied by a soft whimper as she struggled to caress my back and my hair. Fighting against my pants, she dunked her hands right through my zipper and reached for my hard cock. When she found it, she played with my hardened shaft until I could no longer stand.

Tightening my grip on her hips, I slowly walked to my king-sized bed, laid her comfortably on it, and took off my pants completely. I watched her groan silently at the sight of my erect shaft, making me eager to fuck her right then.

Lowering myself in between her legs, I dragged off her

clothes and took one of her perky nipples into my mouth again while my other finger reached down between her legs. Nina gasped as she raised her hand to clutch her other boobs, the sight of which was enough to drive me insane.

My mind raced back to our first time together, and I wondered if it had been this passionate. I wondered if I'd been a gentleman with her or if I'd been rough.

Lifting her legs up by the thigh, I drove right into her, and as I felt her completely.

"This is amazing," I whispered, and she smiled shyly while wriggling her hips and looking deep into my eyes. I couldn't look away; for a moment, I was hypnotized by those eyes and couldn't do anything else then stare into those eyes as my hips danced over her essence.

Out of the blue, a mischievous smile settled on her lips, and she lifted her ass slightly from the couch, and began swaying her hips faster while her legs wrapped around my waist, drawing me deeper into her.

I shot her a wicked smile as understanding crept into my mind. I pulled out slowly, hoping that would torture her to insanity, and as she widened up for better penetration, I plunged into her with a hard, knee-jerking thrust that caused her to gag.

"Fuck! That's so good!" She squealed.

"Oh, you feel so good, baby." I groaned, feeling the mountain of emotion swell up with want like I wasn't having enough.

I felt my nerves shake violently with each thrust. *Fuck!* This was never the case with Lily. In fact, with Lily, it was more of a lust to satisfy my raging sexual desire, but with Nina, it was passion and to equally satisfy her. I guess that is the difference when you're making love to someone you have feelings for.

Nina squirmed and cussed, and her toes curled as pleasure ratcheted, claiming her body in a nerve-jolting release.

"Fuck! More, Will. More, please!" She begged; as my pace increased, several moans escaped her lips, and her breathing slowly grew shallow while streaks of sweat gathered on her temple.

Soon, neither of us could conceal the fire as we both rocked our hips, aiming for the pleasure of our intimacy.

When it was all over, we lay beside each other, allowing our minds to roam freely while we found comfort in each other's company. There was still so much between us that was unsaid, and I needed to address that.

"I'm sorry, Nina. I would never do anything to hurt you." I confessed; my voice muffled from how close I was to her body.

She hesitated for a second and then pulled herself from my embrace.

"I won't deny that I was mad at you, Will." She started, with her back facing me. "Mad that you didn't find me trustworthy enough to tell me about yourself, but now I see why." She said with a smirk.

Phew, this was simple than I'd envisioned. I was expecting tantrums, rattles, and lots of cusses, but Nina was just amazing. She was way more logical and smarter for her age; it was part of the reason I was so attracted to her.

I was about to wrap my arms around her when she scowled, "However, that's not an excuse to keep secrets anymore." She added, turning to glare at me.

"I promise." I said, swallowing a lump of saliva in fear. "Women can be really scary when they're mad at you. One question though, where do you women lend your scary looks from?" I asked, and we both burst out laughing.

"That's funny."

"I'm serious. One minute you ladies are sweet, and affectionate, and the next, you're out for attack. How do you guys switch so fast?" I asked, and watched Nina shake with laughter at the question.

"Story for another day, sweetheart." She replied.

"Or maybe you can tell me over lunch?" I offered.

"Who's preparing lunch?" She asked with a genuine smile.

"I will."

"You cook?" She asked, completely caught off guard.

"See. Now, that is something you just learned about me. I can, indeed, cook." I asked, matching her curiosity.

"I'd never imagined Will Nicholas in the kitchen. What if you forgot you hadn't added seasoning, or you just blackout?" Nina asked, with a scoff before continuing, "You would set the house on fire!" She finished, laughing with enthusiasm at her own jokes while I pretended to be annoyed by her comment.

"I'm sorry. Did I hurt you?" She apologized, drawing next to me on the bed. Nudging on my shoulder, she palmed my face with her right hand and looked into my eyes, worry draining the laughter from her face.

"I didn't mean it that way, I promise. I was just being silly." She continued.

"Mhm. I'll let it slide on one condition." I say to get her attention.

"Yes?"

"You do the dishes!" I laughed.

"What? No! You hired me to be a doctor, not a dishwasher!" Nina protested.

"And I'm the patient. Do I need to remind you that I'm in need of care here?" I asked, trying to win the pointless argument.

"Were you even offended by my joke?" Nina asked, making a puppy face, which was cute.

I couldn't resist it as I bulged, "No. I only saw it as an opportunity to pin the dishes on you." I confessed with a laugh.

"That's better because I have no reason to do the dishes anymore. The punishment is off, and I'm free." She adds, quickly.

"What?"

"You said it yourself, so I'm free." Nina answered, trailing her clothes on the floor, and putting them back on.

"That's you being manipulative!" I yelled, playfully.

"No, that's me following in your footsteps." She mocked, a maniacal laugh erupting from her throat.

"Come on." I coaxed, following closely behind her as we walked out of the bedroom to the kitchen. We moved down the flight of stairs, past my study, but Nina stopped to admire the flowers in my grandfather's supposed garden.

"This flower... what is it called?" Nina asked, sniffing a particular flower from the bunch.

"It's a cosmic flower." I said, replaying the number of times my grandfather had lectured people about it. "It used to be his favorite." I said, my heart growing heavy from the memory.

Nina observed the shift in my mood and came to stand by me.

"I'm sorry, Will. It must have been really difficult, losing the last of your family member." She consoled.

"I always had Freddy, and now, I have you now." I said, planting a kiss on her lips.

"Oh yeah. I ain't going nowhere." She responded with a laugh, returning my kiss.

"Speaking of leaving, why did you go?" I asked. The

question had lingered in my mouth long enough, and I needed to find out.

She blinked and wriggled free from my embrace. With a deep exhale, she wrapped her hands around herself and stood with her back to me again. Seconds merged, and soon we'd been waiting for a minute, but no word had left her mouth.

"Wait, what's that?" She asked, and I took it as her way of changing the subject.

"You shouldn't avoid a question by playing smart, you know." I snapped.

"I'm not trying to play smart here." She snapped back, fondling the flower vase. I watched her struggle with the weight of the vase to no avail.

Slowly I pulled her by the hand and lifted the flower vase from the table, and there it was.

A small piece of brown paper, the color of the vase. It looked like it was used as a mat for the envelope, which must have been why it was difficult to notice, but it'd been there all along. That could only be grandfathers. He usually kept envelopes like that in his office. With fingers trembling, I snatched the paper from the table and flipped it over.

In grandfathers writing, it read:

MY DEAR GRANDSON,
The serpent has an accomplice.

15

The devil you seek lives in your household.

Nina and I exchanged glances, and it was obvious we were thinking the same thing.

"If you can connect the dots, then you'll know why I left." She said, sparing me a serious look.

"Natasha?" I asked, the feeling of guilt biting me.

Just then, my voice beeped, and we both glanced at the caller.

CHAPTER 16

Nina

I know how many days it takes to pitch an idea and how difficult starting a project can be, but if Natasha was ready to shoot this shot, then she must have had the devil backing her up.

"What'd she say?" I asked Will as he dropped the call. He didn't reply immediately, but the smug look on his face was enough to tell me what was going on.

"Natasha wants to meet up."

"Why?" I asked.

"She says she needs to apologize for everything she's done."

"Apologize? That's a trap, Will." I belched, "She must have something up her sleeves. The Natasha I know doesn't seem like someone who would want to apologize." I said, vehemently.

Will was silent for a while, finding out the odds, I suppose.

"It won't take long, I promise. It will be a short meeting." He said after a long pause, and I thought I'd heard something else.

"Are you crazy? She's the devil in disguise here; can't you see that it's a trap?" I pleaded.

Turning to focus on me, Will placed his two hands on my shoulder and patted them gently.

"I know Natasha well enough, and I know how to deal with her."

"Where are you two meeting? I'm coming along!" I said, more of a statement than a request.

"You can't, but you'll do me a favor, okay baby?" Will said, acting like he already had an edge over Natasha. "Get the cops, and meet us at my condo in East Girard, can you do that?" He asked.

"Mhmm." I replied in disappointment. Will smiled down at me and planted a kiss on my cheeks.

"I love you, Nina." He said, with a full smile.

"I love you, too," I replied, scared out of my wit for him, as we stormed out of the house.

Walking to my car, I watched Will unlock his car and spin around to glance at me with an expression on his face that was hard to decipher.

"Hey, be careful." I muttered breathlessly, and he beamed a half smile at me and drove past.

I stared at his car until he was safely out of the gate, then I unlocked mine, dialed Will's Attorney's number, and sped off to the police headquarters.

"Nina! Hello! Is everything alright?" Lawson asked in his airy voice.

"It's not me, it's Will." I answered. That was such a terrific way to get someone worked up.

"What do you mean it's about Will? What's wrong with him?" Lawson asked, his voice on edge.

"Natasha called." I narrated, trying to steady my voice and drive safely at the same time. "She wants Will to meet her at his condo in East Girard; she says she wishes to apologize, but I just feel like there's more. I don't want to sound like I'm being paranoid, but I just don't want him facing her alone." I was already breathless by the time I completed the sentence.

"Where are you?" Lawson simply asked.

"Heading to the police station as we speak." I replied.

"Are you driving?"

"Yes."

"I'll meet you at the police station. You're not being paranoid; you're only taking precautionary measures. Natasha isn't one to be toyed with." There was a long pause, then I heard an iron clank, and the sound of a bunch of keys.

I heard him roused to his feet, take a few strides, and return to the phone.

"Nina, are you there?"

"Yes."

"Can you drive to my office? I could grab some men to go with you there." He offered.

"Perfect." I replied and hung up.

I took a deep breath and steered without even thinking, dashing into the next lane. I heard my tires as they screeched loudly, begging for mercy, but it landed on deaf ears.

I drove like a mad man, and when I arrived at his chamber, Lawson was already waiting outside with his battalion of knights, and I was grateful.

"Thank you so much for agreeing to assist us." I told Lawson as I drew closer.

"Of course. Will deserves peace, and if driving out with you to sabotage Natasha's plans will make that happen, then let's do it." He replied and got into the car next to me.

His envoy of cops roamed into their van, and we all drove out, all roads leading to East Girard.

"There's something you should know, Lawson." I started, deciding whether it was right to disclose what I had to say.

"I'm listening." Lawson replied, his eyes on me.

I grabbed the wheel firmly and exhaled deeply. "I don't know, but I think Natasha killed Will's grandfather." I said and turned to look at him. His eyes didn't blink, and he stared at me like there was more.

"It all makes sense now." He said after a while.

"What does?" I asked, feeling lost and out of the loop.

"You know the drama started after Natasha moved out, and Lily moved in. The bitch didn't want to get her hands dirtied, so she planted a spy to do her bidding. I give it to Lily," Lawson said with a mischievous smile. "... she did a great job, but not such a great one during the hearing."

"Is Will going to be okay?" I asked, withdrawing his attention from Natasha and her minion.

"Depends on how fast we get there." He replied honestly, and I increased the pressure on the gas pedal.

∽

THE PIERCING SOUND of a gun echoed in the distance and the blade slap whirl of a helicopter was enough to tell us that we were driving into danger.

At the sound of the gunshot, the cops dispersed as if it were sounds like a call to action. Each cop jumped out of the van and found a hiding spot while I zoomed back to avoid getting in the way.

"Stay in the car." Lawson warned, as he opened a black envelope, revealing a smooth Glock 9.

"The hell I am! I'm coming with you." I protested.

"No, Nina, it's dangerous out there." He said, detaching the cartridge, and reloading.

"How about you? You're no cop." I said, beginning to unbuckle my seat belt, but Lawson stopped me from proceeding.

"Neither are you." He replied, and then softening, "Listen Nina, there's going to be lots of bullets flying in the air. For Will's sake, don't come out." He warned before leaving.

It was going to be difficult sitting still and doing nothing while Will weathered the storms alone. Restless, I brisked out of the car and dunked my head first behind the police van, and then beside the gate of the condo. I'd never explored the place, so I had a vague idea of the architecture of the building. I stood at the gate, confused. I knew the helicopter was on the rooftop of the thirteen-story building, but I had zero knowledge of how to get there, so I spun around and whisked back to the car.

I didn't need to bother for long when two cops ran head-long with a casualty, but it wasn't Will.

"Sekoni?" I gasped, as I noticed the blood oozing out of his wound; he'd been shot just a few inches from the midbrain.

"Someone call an ambulance!" One of the fighters ordered.

"On it." The second responded.

"Where's Will?" I asked one of the cops who brought Sekoni, as I struggled to wrap a drape over Sekoni's wound, but there was no response. "You'll be fine." I assured him.

Good thing the bullet didn't hit any major artery, I thought as I performed simple first aid.

"What happened up there?" I asked, but Sekoni was too exhausted to say a word.

There was a ceasefire, and soon, some of the cops swarmed out, victory boldly written on their faces, yet no sign of Will or Lawson.

Leaving Sekoni in the car alone, I dashed towards the cops, hoping for an explanation, but no one spared me a glance. I felt a deep surge of anger build up in my bones as I dashed towards the gate, and there I understood why Will and Lawson hadn't left with the others.

Freddy...

The gate spurned open again, and the two men walked out of the gate with Freddy in Will's arms. Then, the remaining cops returned with Natasha, and her men, handcuffs in hand.

Natasha shot me a watch-your-back stare as the cop led her away into their van and drove off.

"He isn't hurt, just in shock." I announced as the ambulance arrived and took the casualties away. Will replied, smiling. "How's Sekoni?"

"In pain." I replied.

"I need him alive, Nina. He stuck out his neck for me."

"What do you mean?" I asked, completely confused about what he meant.

"The helicopter... Natasha's intention was to bomb the plane with Freddy and I in it. Well, Sekoni inactivated the bomb."

"How'd he know about her plan?" I asked, trying to piece every detail together.

"Because he was in Natasha's team on Will's command." Lawson revealed.

"Keep Sekoni alive, Nina." Will repeated, clutching Freddy as I ignited the engine.

～

THE MORNING SUN streaming into the room fell on the flowers by his bed, and they shivered, bathing in the heat. I took another look at the delicate figure coiled up in the bed and smiled. Freddy will have a solid story to tell as he ages, I thought as I shut the door of his room.

Hovering over to my office, I swung the door open and was met with a presence.

"Too early to admit patients?" The man teased without turning around.

"Never too early to admit in-patients." I responded as I sat next to him.

He rose to his feet, wrapped his arms around my waist, and lifted me onto the table before locking his lips with mine. The feeling of his lips against mine filled my body with a happy sensation.

"Sekoni's fine, and ready to leave, and so is Freddy." I announced after he broke the kiss.

"And you, now you have your facility and life back on track, are you ready to come live with me?" Will asked, his eyes feasting on my lips.

"Depends on what that means." I said, playing with his hair and smiling.

"You know what I mean." He says with a smirk.

"No, I don't. That can mean a lot of things, like warm your bed." I threw at him, and he burst out laughing.

"It could also mean marrying me." Will said and dropped to his knees, and I gasped.

"Nina Ross, will you marry me?" He asked, with all the seriousness and love he could muster.

Seeing the look in his eyes, I had no doubt that he was the one, so I nodded, and he placed the beautiful oval shaped, diamond ring on my finger.

"You've made me so happy, Will." I squealed, and we both laughed heartily.

Will planted a deep kiss on my forehead when he stood up again. At that moment, I knew that I found the man for me.

The END

Made in the USA
Columbia, SC
25 March 2024